ACKNOWLEDGMENTS

As with *Unicorn Precinct*, the reissue of *Dragon Precinct*, and the forthcoming *Gryphon Precinct* and *Tales from Dragon Precinct*, the greatest amount of gratitude has to go to Neal Levin of Dark Quest Books for continuing to publish this series. Thanks also to Elektra Hammond for once again doing a fine editing job.

Jahna Romano is a very bright young woman, and an aspiring writer, and she worked on a novel for National Novel Writing Month in 2011. Partly by way of encouraging her, and partly so I would get my own ass in gear, I made *Goblin Precinct* my NaNoWriMo project. The mutual encouragement between self and Jahna was very cool.

Several of the usual suspects: GraceAnne Andreassi DeCandido, Laura Anne Gilman, Dale Mazur, Tina Randleman, and Wrenn Simms, for all-around wonderfulness and support.

Finally, thanks to all those that live with me—human, feline, and canine—for everything.

GOBLIN PRECINCT

GOBLIN PRECINCT

Keith R.A. DeCandido

Dark Quest, LLC
Howell, New Jersey

PUBLISHED BY
Dark Quest, LLC
Neal Levin, Publisher
23 Alec Drive,
Howell, New Jersey 07731
www.darkquestbooks.com

Copyright ©2012, Keith R.A. DeCandido

ISBN (trade paper): 978-1-937051-41-9

Interior Design: Danielle McPhail
Sidhe na Daire Multimedia
www.sidhenadaire.com

Cover Art: Jenn Reese
www.tigerbrightstudios.com

Dedicated to the memory of
Wilma Diaz O'Kelley
and Lisa-Karen Hawkins,
both bright lights taken from us too young.

PROLOGUE

ODDLY, GIVEN HOW MISERABLE HE'D BEEN THE PAST FEW YEARS, Elthor lothSerra was happier than he'd ever been in his century-plus of life when he died.

Once, many years ago, Elthor was a member of the Elf Queen's court. He had a charming wife, a beautiful mistress, dozens of servants, hundreds of slaves, all the food he could consume (and then some), and enough gold to drown himself in.

Elthor's wealth was inherited, but he also invested wisely, and one of his concerns was in swordmaking—a boom business during war, and the Elf Queen was always at war with *someone*.

Then, of course, came the biggest war of all, as the Elf Queen tried to extend her grasp to all the dwarven and human lands. And she would have succeeded, too, had it not been for the betrayal of her nephew, Olthar lothSirhans.

Elthor had always considered Olthar to be a dear friend and comrade. His betrayal had stung at the time.

Said betrayal was the beginning of the end for the Elf Queen, which meant it was also the end for Elthor. His fortunes were tied entirely to his being a favorite of the Elf Queen, and when things took a turn for the worse, his own lifespan—once guaranteed to last a couple of centuries—was now measured in hours.

Unless, of course, he got out. He had sufficient cash reserves, and barely enough people who thought highly of him, to get out of the elven lands. When the Elf Queen was brought down by human soldiers led by the legendary Gan Brightblade, Elthor was long gone.

Olthar, for all that he and Brightblade had become comrades, was not among those who brought the Elf Queen down. Indeed, he never set foot in elven lands again after his betrayal. Up until his own hasty departure, Elthor had thought that to be cowardly.

But how could he go home after leaving in ignominy? For decades, he had traveled in lavish coaches drawn by the finest horses. When he left home, for what turned out to be the last time, it was hiding in a merchant's carriage drawn by one slow, elderly horse. He was surrounded by assorted badly packed dry goods and the ride east nearly destroyed his back.

Finding somewhere to go proved more problematic than he had first thought. In the past, all he'd had to do was say he was a member of the Elf Queen's court and he could stay in the best accommodations with serving staff at his beck and call. Now, the very mention of a connection to the Elf Queen would like as not put him on the wrong end of a sword. With his luck, it would be a blade made by one of his own swordmasters.

Eventually, he found himself in the city-state of Cliff's End. A nominally human metropolis—it was run by Lord Albin and Lady Meerka, who served the human king and queen—it was, in fact, an incredibly diverse place where elves, dwarves, gnomes, and halflings mingled with humans with little difficulty or revulsion.

Elthor had been pretty disgusted when he arrived, but given his current station in life, he wasn't in a position to be fussy. And the ease of blending in proved useful.

He had come to the port city with the thought of hiring a boat to one of the islands on the Garamin Sea where they didn't ask questions, but by the time he arrived, he'd gone through all his cash reserves, with poor lodgings eating through his remaining coin in a week's time.

Only a year after escaping his home with his life, Elthor lothSerra found himself reduced to begging on Haven's Lane. It was his only option, as being a nobleman for a great empire left one without very many marketable skills. His attempts at securing employment proved pathetic and short-lived.

So he begged. And grew more and more unhappy.

As the years passed—Elthor honestly had no idea how many, as his sense of time had atrophied from lack of caring—he got progressively better at begging and proportionately more unhappy.

One of the other beggars he occasionally shared space with on Haven's Way was a gnome whose name Elthor had never bothered to learn. On one occasion, the gnome asked Elthor, "Why aint'cha happy?"

Elthor just stared at him. "Are you mad? What could I possibly be *happy* about?"

"What ain't there t'be happy about?" The gnome shook his head. "This is the life, innit? You sit around all day and people just throw coins at you for lookin' pathetic. Shit, all's you have to be doin' is lookin' like your usual self, and it's good for a couple gold a day. What could be better?"

"Almost anything."

The gnome laughed and shook his head. "You gotcherself entirely the wrong attitude, you do. Know whatcha need?"

"A boat to take me away from this cesspit of a city?"

"Naw, you're needed somethin' for cheer. An' I know someone's got just the thing."

Elthor had ignored the gnome for the rest of the day, but on the next, he offered Elthor a pill.

"What is this?" Elthor asked, pointedly not taking the proffered item.

"It's called 'Bliss.' It'll put the smile back on your face, it will. Just costs a copper."

At first, Elthor was going to reject the gnome's offer out of hand. After all, he was truly endeavoring to save up to hire that boat.

But how realistic a notion was that? He'd been begging for years now, and—once he'd spent what he needed for food, drink, and the occasional awful accommodation, usually during winter—he'd only scraped together a few gold. While he'd attempted to keep his personal spending down, it still wasn't enough. He'd been absolutely ruthless in paring his spending down. Indeed, the only time he'd indulged himself was to buy a celebratory drink when he heard the news that Olthar lothSirhans had been killed.

He was decades away from even considering the possibility of hiring a boat, and he was fairly sure that he'd go completely mad long before then.

There was also the stark realization that the only day he'd been truly happy since coming to this city-state was the day he learned that Olthar had been murdered. On that day, his only sadness was that he had not been the one to wield the weapon that killed the betrayer.

So, at once both reluctant and eager, Elthor took the pill that the gnome offered in exchange for a copper recently dropped in his hat by one of his regulars.

At first, nothing changed, and Elthor was about to demand his copper back—then suddenly he was utterly suffused with joy! The sun, formerly an unwelcome intrusion of light, was now bright and lovely! The stinks of Haven's Way became pleasurable, the drab colors of Goblin Precinct's buildings became bright and vivid, and the sussurus of the downtrodden voices of the Cliff's End poor became a symphony of noise!

For the first time since Olthar's betrayal, Elthor truly felt joy!

The day passed by quickly, and Elthor got many fewer coins than usual—after all, who would give money to so happy a beggar?—but he found that he didn't care.

At least until roughly sundown, when it all just stopped. The scents became odors once more, the noise became oppressive, the sights dull. As miserable as he'd been before taking Bliss, it was as nothing compared to how he felt now, with the knowledge that such transcendent happiness had been his just minutes ago.

His sleep was troubled, his dreams filled with images of people he hadn't seen in years, but the most prominent was Olthar lothSirhans, laughing at him.

The next morning, he sought out the gnome and bought a dozen of the Bliss pills, figuring they would keep him going for a week or so.

But the second pill only lasted a few hours, and the third only two. With each pill, the high was of a shorter duration, the crash harder and nastier. It got to the point where Elthor was taking a pill every quarter-hour, desperate to maintain the joy and stave off the doom.

One morning, the gnome, whose name was Chobral, wandered into Haven's Way to inquire as to whether or not Elthor wanted more pills, only to find that he lay dead in the alley.

With a sigh at losing a paying customer—Chobral got twenty percent of the take from any direct sales he made, and Elthor had the makings of a good regular—the gnome went to find a member of the Cliff's End Castle Guard to report the dead body.

ONE

As usual, Lieutenant Torin ban Wyvald of the Cliff's End
Castle Guard was late. His half-elf, half-human partner, Lieutenant
Danthres Tresyllione, knew he never had a good excuse, and after
a decade of partnership, she had ceased trying to come up with bad
ones to give Sergeant Jonas. For his part, Jonas didn't bother waiting for Torin to start the morning rundown. Torin and Danthres
were two of six detectives on the day shift of the Guard, and they
were tasked with solving the more complex crimes committed
within the demesne.

"We've had at least three reported Bliss overdoses in Goblin
overnight," Jonas was saying as Danthres stared at Torin's empty
chair. Their desks abutted in the squadroom located at the eastern
wing of the Lord and Lady's castle.

Iaian snorted as he leaned back in his chair. "Only three?
They're slipping."

His much younger partner, Amilar Grovis, looked disgusted.
"It's a tragedy, is what it is! People dying from ingestion of such
foul substances! It's an affront to Ghandurha!" Grovis then made
the hand gestures that devotees of his god tended to make whenever
they were appalled by the behavior of nonbelievers. Danthres had
seen Grovis make that gesture with tiresome regularity. "Something," the young lieutenant added, "should be done about it."

"Like what?" Lieutenant Hawk asked. He was sitting on the side
of his partner Lieutenant Dru's desk, the latter facing him from his
chair. "If people want to be killing themselves, why should we stop
'em?"

Iaian nodded. "You try to legislate how people behave, you're gonna have more criminals than the hole can hold."

"In any event," Jonas said, "Goblin's got a detail taking the bodies to the shop." Any corpses that were unlikely to be claimed by a relative or friend were taken to the shop, a cave just outside the city-state's walls where they were disposed of. From what Danthres understood, they'd been backed up, thanks to Bliss's new prevalence adding to the unwanted dead. "Dru, Hawk, you two are done with the Corvin case, yes?"

Both lieutenants visibly shuddered at that. "Finally, yeah."

Jonas nodded, shuffling parchments. "Fine, you're up next, then. We've got—"

The door flew open, and Danthres looked over, hoping it would be her partner. Instead, it was one of the guards assigned to the castle. Because of that, his leather armor, like that of Jonas and all the detectives in the room, had a gryphon crest on the chest. His lack of a cloak indicated that he merely held the rank of guard, which, as far as Danthres was concerned, meant she could ignore him as much as possible. She certainly wasn't about to be bothered enough to learn his name.

"There's been a robbery, like!" the guard said breathlessly. "One'a th'youth squad just came with a message sayin' the main branch'a the Cliff's End Bank's been robbed, like!"

Grovis rose to his feet, his face twisted into outrage. His father was the president of the bank in question, which was the largest money house in Cliff's End, with four locations across the city-state. In a just world, Grovis himself would be working under his father, but the elder Grovis wanted his eldest son to join the Castle Guard to "make a man of him." It was the considered opinion of the other lieutenants in the squadroom—especially Grovis's long-suffering partner, Iaian—that Grovis didn't have the materials necessary for such a manufacture.

"*Been* robbed?" Grovis asked. "You mean they've gotten away with it?"

The guard nodded, and Danthres asked no one in particular, "That's the first time the bank's been successfully robbed, isn't it?"

"Indeed it is," Grovis said gravely.

Jonas looked over at Dru and Hawk. "You two have it."

Whirling on the sergeant, Grovis bellowed, "What!? It's my *father's* bank! I practically grew up in that building! I *must* be the one to investigate it!"

"Dru and Hawk are up," Jonas said, "and you're too close to the investigation to be objective."

"The hell does being objective matter?" Iaian asked incredulously.

"So you agree with me," Grovis said triumphantly.

"Not hardly. Dru and Hawk're up, let them deal with it." Iaian was only a couple of years from being in the Guard for twenty-five years, thus vesting his pension, and Danthres was of the opinion that his intent was to make as little effort as possible in those final years.

Hawk and Dru had gotten to their feet, and the former put a hand on Grovis's shoulder. "Don't you be worrying. We'll find out who hit Daddy's bank."

"I am less than comforted," Grovis muttered.

"You have a problem with the standard policy of the Castle Guard," Jonas said pointedly, "you can take it up with Captain Osric."

Dru and Hawk put on their earth-colored cloaks of office and then followed the guard out the door. Grovis just stood in the middle of the squadroom, looking even more like a fish than usual.

Danthres had to admit to enjoying the sight of Grovis so flustered.

Torin ban Wyvald came ambling into the grand entrance to the castle approximately a quarter-hour past when he was supposed to be there. He had simply not left himself enough time to get ready after waking up—just like most mornings. The notion of getting up earlier had been considered and rejected many times. Torin was always sure that *this* morning, he'd be able to get ready faster.

Ten years of being wrong had yet to cure him of this particular hope.

The castle's entrance was large enough to fit a troll standing on another troll's shoulders, and wide enough for two coaches. It also had a metal portcullis and massive wooden double doors that were nigh-impenetrable back in the day. After all, Cliff's End had once been just the castle, which was located near a valuable port.

Upon entering, Torin heard an uncommon sound: Captain Osric's laughter.

In the days of the elven wars, Torin had served as a soldier under Osric. When he came to Cliff's End, Osric was the head of the Castle Guard, and offered Torin a position there as a detective.

To hear the sullen Osric laugh was bizarre to say the least. Having lost an eye in the war, Osric wore a silk eyepatch and cultivated dark stubble on his cheeks, giving him the look of a man who would cut your throat as soon as talk to you. Torin couldn't even recall the last time Osric had smiled.

He came into view around a corner, headed in the same direction as Torin: toward the eastern wing and the squadroom. With him was an elf wearing battered leather armor, with a scar on one cheek, short dirty blond hair, and a thick blond mustache. Most elves Torin had encountered tried to magic away scars—whether via healing potion or a glamour. The only ones who had facial hair were usually the type who would proudly wear scars.

This was a soldier. And he looked familiar, though Torin couldn't quite place him.

The captain then said words Torin had never heard him use before in sequence, "Ah, ban Wyvald, glad to see you."

"Captain."

"Fanthral, this is Lieutenant Torin ban Wyvald. Once, he was one of my worst soliders, and now he is one of my best detectives. Ban Wyvald, this is General Fanthral—well, just Fanthral, now. Remember him, from the war?"

Torin nodded, his face flushing with an unexpected anger. "Of course. The Midwinter Game."

Fanthral had been a general in service to the Elf Queen. One midwinter, he and Osric were on opposite ends of the Nemerian Wastes. The snow and ice were vicious, and everyone was huddled in tents that were woefully inadequate to protect them from the elements. Fanthral's troops were equally frozen, and since fighting was out of the question, the two sides started actually talking. At first it was the expected insults, but it soon modulated into giving each other advice on staying warm. After a day, they started playing games with improvised balls and cards that people had around.

Three months later, when things went badly for the Elf Queen, Fanthral took the side of Olthar lothSirhans's rebels, and specifically surrendered himself to Osric—he wouldn't do so to any other human general.

Osric looked at Fanthral. "Torin here was one of the few who was able to buck the troops up. He seemed utterly unaffected by the cold."

"Two winters previous," Torin said, "I was alone and armorless in the Forest of Orven."

Fanthral seemed to actually notice Torin for the first time. "The wastes must have seemed a summer retreat by comparison."

Torin nodded. "In any event, General, yes, I do remember you. And the condition in which your prisoners were given back to us when we had our exchange."

The elf's face darkened. "We had little choice."

"Really? You were *forced* to cut off fingers and gouge out eyes?"

"In fact, Lieutenant, we were. The Elf Queen was very specific with her standing orders in how to treat human prisoners—and how those who did not follow those orders were to be punished. Both had the same result."

Relenting a bit, Torin said, "I suppose." But he recalled in particular one of his dearest friends, Ellek, who died shortly after Fanthral returned him. The once ebullient and charming young man was silent and depressed when he was brought back, and died quietly soon after.

Not wishing to dwell on this subject, Torin asked, "What brings you to Cliff's End now, sir?"

Fanthral started to answer, but Osric cut him off. "Let's continue to the squadroom—everyone needs to hear this." The captain's smile had fallen and he was back to his trademark scowl.

Torin didn't find that, or his words, particularly comforting.

Glancing back at the large entrance as they proceeded, Fanthral asked, "When was the last time the castle doors were shut?"

Osric also turned to look at them briefly before they went on. "Not since I came here, certainly. Even in winter, they're left open to the elements—the interior doors keep the castle warmed."

"The portcullis and doors," Torin said, "are an artifact of the days when this castle was regularly attacked. That is no longer the case."

Fanthral snorted. "All the more reason to be prepared. The portcullis is no doubt rusted and pitted, and I suspect the same to be true of the doors' hinges. If you were to be invaded now—"

"We would see them coming," Torin said. "When the gate was in use, sir, invading armies came under cover of the Forest of Nimvale. As Cliff's End has grown, the border of that forest has moved considerably back from right upon the castle, and there are also half-a-dozen wide pathways that have been cleared to allow easy access to the city-state."

Now Osric smirked. "Remember when I said that ban Wyvald was one of my worst soldiers? It was because he thought far too much. But it's also why I count him among my two finest detectives."

"Good," Fanthral said gravely, causing Torin to again wonder what this was all about.

The three of them entered the squadroom just as Dru and Hawk were leaving.

"Cap'n," Dru said. "Someone robbed the Cliff's End Bank."

Osric nodded. "Get to it."

Torin followed the captain and the elf into the squadroom. Grovis was standing in the center of the room looking piscine as usual, Jonas standing nearby shuffling parchments, while Iaian and Danthres were seated at their desks.

"About time you got here," Danthres said playfully to Torin. A small smile formed on her oddly constructed face, which combined the less fortunate elements of her dual heritage. "We were about to send the hounds."

Allowing a grin to show through his thick red beard, Torin said, "Don't be absurd. You don't even notice that I'm not here until half an hour past the start of shift."

"True." Danthres's smile fell. "Who's your friend?"

Osric answered her question. "This is Fanthral, a representative of the Elven Consortium."

Iaian snorted. "Is *that* what they're callin' the latest buncha ne'er-do-wells tryin' to keep the elves under control?"

Archly, Fanthral said, "The Consortium is currently engaged in war trials against those who supported the Elf Queen."

"A dozen years, and they're just now getting to the trials?" Iaian shook his head, his arms folded across the gryphon symbol on his armor's chestplate.

Now Fanthral smiled mirthlessly. "My people do not leap headlong into things."

Torin found himself unable to resist. "That would explain why you took so long to renounce the Elf Queen after fighting for her cause for so long."

Fanthral glared at Torin, and Osric scowled. Torin pointedly ignored both looks, choosing instead to focus on Danthres's approving gaze. Indeed, it was the sort of thing Danthres might have said, and Torin found himself reminded, not for the first time, of how much his partner was rubbing off on him.

"I have been deputized by the Consortium," Fanthral said after another moment of glaring, "to seek out Elthor lothSerra, who was a member of the Elf Queen's court." Reaching into a pouch on his belt, he pulled out a dark blue gem. "This gem allowed me to track him to Cliff's End, but after my arrival within these walls, the gem went dark. Within the region that Osric tells me is Goblin Precinct, I was able to determine that an elf matching lothSerra's description was found dead."

Danthres leaned forward. "That's gonna make it hard to put him on trial."

"Indeed it is, halfbreed." Fanthral sneered the words.

Torin sighed. Elves thought very little of those of their kind who bred with "inferiors," and that was as nothing compared to how poorly they regarded the resultant offspring.

Holding out his hands, Iaian asked, "What the hell does any of this have to do with us?"

Osric answered. "The guards in Goblin assumed lothSerra to be another beggar on Haven's Way who overdosed on Bliss. His body's already been sent to the shop."

"That," Danthres said, "would appear to be that."

"Hardly." Fanthral was still sneering. "It is quite possible that lothSerra was targeted. There are many among the elven elders who do not wish these trials to go forward, who fear what people like lothSerra will testify to when put on trial."

Torin said, "If this gentleman was found on Haven's Way, he had fallen quite far from his previous station. He would be far from the first beggar to take too much Bliss."

"This week," Danthres added.

"And the people who wish these trials stopped do have resources," Fanthral said insistently. "They could just as easily have made lothSerra's death seem like a simple beggar's overdose precisely because they knew there would be no investigation, the body destroyed."

"Luckily," Osric said, "the shop is backed up. His body might still be there. Tresyllione, ban Wyvald, you're to escort Fanthral to the shop and see if you can use his gem to find lothSerra's corpse."

"Within a certain proximity," Fanthral added, "it can detect him even if he is no longer alive."

Torin did not relish the notion of spending any more time with this man, but said nothing.

His partner, predictably, was less reticent. "You want us to go corpse-diving—with *him*?"

"For starters, yes." Osric fixed his scowl on Danthres. "Then you will investigate Elthor lothSerra's death just like you would any other possible murder."

"That would require a peel-back of Haven's Way," Torin said. "Has Boneen returned yet?"

"Who's Boneen?" Fanthral asked.

Osric replied: "Our magickal examiner. The Brotherhood of Wizards loaned him to us to perform Inanimate Residue Spells on scenes where crimes have taken place."

Fanthral nodded. "I can see how that would be useful."

For the first time since Torin's arrival, Sergeant Jonas spoke. "It would if he were here. However, he has been at a conference the brotherhood has been holding, and has yet to return, nor give any indication if or when he will."

Chuckling, Iaian said, "Brotherhood's probably all in a tizzy after that mess with Ythran."

Fanthral's eyes went wide. "Lord Ythran?"

"You know him?" Osric asked.

"I know of him. One of the finest wizards."

"No longer," Danthres said with a nasty smile. "He was involved in a scandal involving a false religion in Iaron. Removed from his post as representative of the brotherhood for this region."

"Tresyllione and ban Wyvald were the ones who exposed him," Osric said proudly, "which is why I'm assigning them to you, Fanthral. I know how important it is to the Consortium that the truth behind lothSerra's death be found, and," he added pointedly, "how important it is to the Lord and Lady that Cliff's End's relations with the Consortium remain cordial."

That was the other coin that fell to the floor, as it were. As usual, what made sense took a back seat to political expediency and what Lord Albin and Lady Meerka wanted. It mattered to them that lothSerra's death be fully investigated by Osric's best detectives, and therefore it mattered to Osric, since the Lord and Lady were the ones who hired him and could just as easily get rid of him—or anyone else.

Letting out a very long sigh, Danthres got to her feet, walking over to the pegboard that held her cloak. "All right, then. Let's go find a body."

Osric, however, was staring at Grovis, who, at some point, had sat back down at his desk. "You all right, Grovis? You've been unusually quiet."

"I cannot be*lieve* that someone would just rob my father's bank like that! It's absurd!"

Urgently, Danthres said, "Let's go. I'd rather spend all day in the shop than listen to Grovis's bleating anymore."

Torin smiled. "Of course." He indicated the doorway. "Shall we?"

Fanthral nodded. "We shall. And I hope the pair of you are as good as your captain says you are."

"You thought highly enough of Osric to surrender to him twelve years ago, sir," Torin said tartly.

Danthres added, "So feel free to think just as highly of him now." She shrugged. "Or don't, it matters very little to me."

With that, she left, Fanthral following behind, and Torin behind him.

He just hoped that they hadn't gotten around to incinerating lothSerra's corpse yet.

TWO

DANTHRES SURELY THOUGHT SHE WAS GOING TO GAG AT THE SMELL OF all the corpses. Her only solace came from the fact that, as badly as she was suffering from the odor, it was even worse for Fanthral. Danthres's elven senses were at least dulled by her human half, which today was a blessing.

The body shop was run by a fat dwarf named Orvag in a cave located within the Forest of Nimvale. Strictly speaking outside the Lord and Lady's demesne, its distance from the city-state proper was necessary for the olfactory survival of its citizens.

If a corpse lay unclaimed, it was taken by the Castle Guard to the body shop, where it was placed on a pallet. Orvag had fifty pallets, and on a normal day they wouldn't all be filled. The last time Danthres had been here was after a hurricane, when the number of unclaimed dead had skyrocketed. Then, Orvag had doubled up on every pallet, and still had to pile a few on the floor.

This time was far worse than after the hurricane. Each pallet was tripled up, and there were two tangles of bodies in the corners of the cavern.

On the far end of the cavern was a massive firepit, in which Orvag disposed of the bodies. While enclosed from the rest of the cavern by stone walls, the firepit did open upward to the sky, protecting Orvag and his workers from the worst of the heat, but it also made approaching the shop impossible to do without breathing through your mouth.

Her leather-armored arm held in front of her face, Danthres turned to look at her partner. "Torin, remember that house that had the closet explode with all the muck from half of Cliff's End bursting out of it?"

Torin nodded.

"I wish this place smelled as good as that."

That got a chuckle out of Torin and another sneer from Fanthral. The latter said, "May we please get this over with?"

Orvag approached them, his soot-stained face breaking into a massive grin. He wore an apron that had even more soot stains than his face—he'd actually washed the face some time in the past year, which was more than could be said for the apron—and carried a huge poker that was half again as long as the dwarf was tall. "Well well well! What brings the Cloaks into my place'a business, eh?"

"We're looking for a body," Torin said.

"Well, you've come to the right place, eh?" Orvag laughed heartily. "Any one in particular, or you just want one I pick at random, eh?"

"This is *not* a joking matter." Fanthral's tone was bitter. "We seek the corpse of Elthor lothSerra, and you'd best pray to whatever foul deities your diminutive kind worships that you haven't yet incinerated it."

Orvag's laughter modulated into a frown. "I don't know who you are, eh? But you ain't wearin' no castle guard uniform, so I ain't have to take such tone from you."

Fanthral stepped forward, and Orvag tightened his grip on his poker.

Danthres would have been more than happy to just sit back and watch them go at it—she especially was curious as to where, exactly Orvag might stick the poker—but Torin intervened, ruining her fun. "Fanthral here is a diplomatic representative from the Elven Consortium."

"I don't give a shit if he's the lord and lady's son, I ain't being spoken to like that in my own place, eh?"

"A charnel house is indeed your 'place,' dwarf." Fanthral continued to move forward.

Then he stopped, looking down at the pouch on his belt, which Danthres noticed was now glowing. Reaching into it, Fanthral pulled out the gem he had shown them in the squadroom, but now it appeared to be lit from within by a light blue flame.

"He's here. Be grateful, dwarf, that you have not yet performed your ministrations upon him."

Orvag gripped the poker tightly. "I'll perform a ministration on you, y—"

"That's enough," Torin said to them both, then asked Fanthral: "Can you pinpoint the body?"

"I believe so." Fanthral walked over toward the pallets, finally finding one that had an elderly male elf and two human females, all covered in grime. "This is Elthor lothSerra."

"He *is* being claimed, eh?" Orvag asked.

"So it would seem," Torin said.

"Fine by me, eh? One less body to deal with—you're welcome to it."

"Good." Fanthral turned to Torin and Danthres. "Please remove the body to wherever it is that your magickal examiner stores them."

Danthres's eyes widened. "Excuse me?"

"Were my words not clear, halfbreed?"

"Oh, I heard you, believe me."

"Then what is the problem?"

Torin cut Danthres off before she could give her incredibly rude answer to the question. "Because, sir, one of the many advantages to our rank of lieutenant is that we are spared such onerous duties as that of hauling corpses hither and yon. We shall summon some guards from the castle, who will take care of it."

Danthres looked at Torin. "All right, I'll admit, you said that better than I would have."

Grinning, Torin said, "Considering that you would have said something along the lines of, 'The problem is that you're a shitbrain,' that wasn't much of an accomplishment."

Returning the grin, Danthres replied, "True." She turned toward the body. "I have to say, Fanthral, that your conspiracy theory is looking less likely."

The elf now stood with his arms folded over his chest, regarding Danthres with unconcealed contempt. "And you *have* to say that, do you?"

Ignoring the dig, Danthres continued. "Your notion is that lothSerra was found by enemies and framed by brigands determined to keep him from his rightful place as the subject of one of your Consortium's trials, yes?"

"I would not have used the term *brigands*, but that is what I believe happened." He walked over toward the corpse as well. "He was no doubt hiding in this city-state, hoping to remain anonymous. People of every race pass through Cliff's End, after all. One more elf would hardly cause comment, and most people here—especially in the poorer region where he was found—keep to themselves. But then he was found by someone working against the Consortium's purpose, and they overfed him this drug you were speaking of, and they placed him in that alley."

Danthres looked at Torin. "Quite an impressive story."

Torin nodded. "It does have a certain ring to it, yes."

"But, unfortunately, it's shit."

Fanthral sneered again. "Excuse me?"

Smiling sweetly, Danthres asked, "Were my words not clear?"

"Do not try my patience, halfbreed. I've come a long way to find—"

"A beggar."

Thrown off by the interruption, Fanthral blinked. "A what?"

"Look at the body, Fanthral." Danthres was now pointing at the corpse. "That isn't dirt and grime that someone put on him to make sure he looked the part. And these clothes, if you can call them that, were practically welded to his person. LothSerra wasn't dressed up to look like a beggar, he *was* a beggar."

"Impossible." Fanthral scoffed and turned away. "He was one of the highest ranking members of the Elf Queen's court. He would rather die than live like that."

"Indeed," Torin said. "Why else do you think he overdosed on Bliss? The drug is fairly new to the city, but from all reports it bestows euphoria upon one. What better pill for an elf lord who has lost everything to swallow?"

Fanthral looked back at the body. "It couldn't be that simple, could it?"

"Yes, it could." Danthres shook her head. "Torin and I have been doing this for some time. In our experience, the simplest explanation is more often than not the right one."

"Perhaps." Fanthral strode toward the exit. "And perhaps not. Your pretty story is no more or less proven than mine, Lieutenants. I believe your captain instructed you to investigate lothSerra's death, and you will do precisely that. Then we will learn which of our stories is the story and which is the truth."

Orvag watched as he departed. "He's an emissary of the elves, eh?"

Danthres nodded.

"No wonder they've gone to shit."

At that, Torin and Danthres both laughed. The former said, "We'll send some guards over for the body forthwith."

"Suit yourselves—I got me more people to burn up, eh?"

"Better you than me," Danthres said emphatically. "C'mon, Torin, let's go so I can breathe through my nose again."

THREE

"YOU'RE KIDDING ME, YOU FOUND A BOAT?"

"Maybe," Hawk said cautiously at his partner's query. "See, this is why I wasn't gonna be tellin' you. You're always jumpin' the gun on me, gettin' all excited when it ain't so yet."

Dru rolled his eyes. "C'mon, Hawk, you been talkin' about getting a boat when you hit your twenty-five. You're sayin' you found one you can afford *now*?"

Hawk repeated, "Maybe. He said he could be givin' it to me for two hundred gold, which is way less than what I thought I'd be payin', and he'll take half now and the rest next year."

Now Dru had a faraway look, and Hawk could almost see his cynicism kicking back in. "There's gotta be somethin' wrong with the boat."

"That's what I was thinkin', too, but I looked it over five times—even paid off that friend'a Horran's down in the docks to check it out, and he said it was ship-shape."

As they turned the corner onto Frannik's Lane toward the main branch of the Cliff's End Bank, Dru asked, "You trust Horran's friend?"

"After payin' him three gold? Yeah, I trust him."

Dru winced. "That's overpayin', ain't it?"

"I wanted an honest assessment, and the guy I'm buyin' from wouldn't be payin' more than that in a counterbribe."

Nodding, Dru said, "Yeah, you're probably right. So, you gonna do it?"

Hawk sighed. "Still not sure. I mean, what's Dad gonna do?"

"Seriously? *That's* your worry? Hawk, your Dad—"

Whatever Dru was going to say about Hawk's Dad was lost to the very tall, very thin man in the tailored suit who met them in the middle of Frannik's Lane in front of the bank.

He had his hands together, fingers interlaced, over his heart as he asked, "Oh, please, for Ghandurha's sake, tell me you're here to investigate the robbery, yes?"

"Yes, sir, we are. I'm Lieutenant Dru, this is my partner, Lieutenant Hawk."

"I'm Than Martel, the manager of this branch. I'm so very glad to see you—this is such a disaster, especially with Mr. Grovis about to be on the rolls! Please, for Ghandurha's sake, tell me you've investigated robberies before, yes?"

"Of course we have, sir." Hawk was surprised he was so outraged at the question. It wasn't like he wasn't asked it every single time he and Dru showed up at a scene. He wondered if Torin and Danthres got the question, too. (Grovis and Iaian probably did, but he'd expect people to be unsure of the pair of *them* on sight.)

Dru added, "I'm sorry, Mr. Martel, but did you say that Harcort Grovis is gonna be made a member of the court?"

"Yes, he told us all last week. Why?" Martel had a very mouse-like face for a man so tall, and now his cheeks were twitching.

"No reason," Dru said, though Hawk assumed his partner was thinking the same thing he was: why hadn't Grovis mentioned that Daddy was being made into Sir Harcort? It was unlike their fish-faced partner to miss a chance to gloat about his family.

Martel clapped his hands once for no obvious reason. "Now, then, I suppose you'll need us to clear the bank. Er, where is your magickal examiner?"

Hawk exchanged glances with Dru. "I'm truly sorry, Mr. Martel," Hawk said, "but our M.E. isn't available. Don't be worryin', though, he'll be back soon, and he can cast the peel-back then. Meantime, we need to be havin' a look 'round."

"I'm sorry, but—well, please, for Ghandurha's sake, tell me what *you're* doing here?"

Angrily, Dru said, "Hey, look, we don't just go where the M.E. points and arrest somebody. The peel-back isn't completely conclusive every time, and sometimes all it tells us is what the perp looks like, not where he is or who he is or anything like that. We still need to do *our* jobs—the M.E. just helps. So if you'd be so kind as to show us into the bank and tell us what happened, we'd be grateful."

"Yes, but—well, you two shouldn't even be the ones handling this case. I mean—well, please, for Ghandurha's sake, tell me that the only reason why Lieutenant Grovis isn't here is because he's on another case."

Without thinking, Hawk said, "Why would we want *him* here?"

"Isn't it obvious?" Martel was now staring with his long face twisted into an expression of shock and disgust. "He *knows* this bank—his father *owns* it, after all. Shouldn't *he* be the one to investigate?"

"Trust me," Hawk muttered, "whatever he knows about the bank is more than made up for by what he don't know about policework."

Martel frowned and moved closer. "I'm sorry, what was that?"

Hawk was about to repeat his insult louder when Dru interrupted. "What my partner means is that Lieutenant Grovis is our least experienced detective. Yes, he knows the bank, but he doesn't have as many years in the job as Lieutenant Hawk and I do."

With a very long sigh, Martel said, "Very well, please do come inside."

The main branch of the Cliff's End Bank was a two-story structure, with the second level being a balcony that ran around the entire edge of the building, still allowing those on the first floor to look up at the ceiling, which was decorated in what was once probably a lovely painting, but which now looked like muddy colors all running together.

Hawk had never been inside the bank before—he preferred to keep his money somewhere safe, like under his bunk—but he figured there were usually more people wandering the marble floor.

The teller stations were empty, and only a few people were on the main floor, and most of them were guards assigned to Dragon Precinct.

Simon, one of the latter, approached. Frannik's Lane was located on the border between Dragon and Unicorn, and Hawk grumbled at Simon's presence at the bank.

"Toldja Dragon'd take the call." Dru was gloating. "You owe me a copper."

"Gimme a break—I got a boat to save up for."

"'Course they came to us," Simon said with a smile. "Youth squad hates goin' to Unicorn. They're shit tippers up there."

"Which is what I told you," Dru said. "So what do we got?"

"Some guys came in and robbed the bank. They had swords and daggers. That's all I know—I saved 'em all for you two."

"How many guys?" Hawk asked.

"No, seriously," Simon said, "that's all I know."

Dru frowned. "So, what, you don't know how many there were?"

"Anywhere between two and fifteen, depending on who you ask."

Hawk sighed. "That's just great."

"S'okay, Boneen'll come by and do the peel-back, right?"

While Dru shook his head, Hawk answered. "Boneen's off on some brotherhood thing. We're stuck with what these upstandin' citizens be seein'."

Simon winced. "Yeah, good luck with that." He pointed at the back area of the bank, and Hawk noticed that there were about two dozen people of various races seated there. None of them looked particularly happy, least of all the four humans wearing suits very similar to that of Martel. Hawk figured them to be the other bank workers.

Hawk looked around and saw two small offices. "What're those?"

"Manager's office," Simon said, "and assistant manager's office."

"Good—we'll be usin' those. I'll take the manager."

Dru folded his arms. "Why do you get the manager's office?"

Shrugging, Hawk said, "What difference does it make?"

"Fine, then let me have the manager's office."

"No."

Dru grinned. "What difference does it make?"

"Because I called it, and because you're bein' all childish." Refusing to even continue this conversation, Hawk turned to Simon. "Send us each one at a time. We'll be takin' their statements."

"Have fun."

Hawk snorted a chuckle and went into the manager's office. Martel certainly worked in comfort: he had a leather chair and a wooden desk that was well polished. A lot better than the pitted monstrosity he had to sit behind in the castle.

Simon sent in the first witness, an elderly elf.

"Well, you see, I'm afraid my eyesight isn't very good, and I'm afraid I didn't see much, but I can tell you that there were three of them and they had longswords—big ones, very sharp. Couldn't see their faces, though—probably magic. Maybe they were wizards?"

Next was a young human woman.

"I saw *everything*! There were five of them, and they had these *really* shitty short swords, I mean they couldn't cut *shit*. And they came in, and they had really cheap-shit glamours. I can tell you they were all human, and wouldn't no good glamour allow you to tell *that*."

Then there was the middle-aged dwarf.

"Only saw some of what was goin' on, but I can tell you this much—there was definitely four of 'em. Had some kind of maces or some such, all three of 'em did, and you couldn't see none of their faces. All five of 'em had masks or some such."

Hawk was about ready to yank all his dreadlocks out by the time he got to the fourth person, a human male.

"Of course I saw what happened. I mean, I know for sure that there were six of them—probably. And they were almost definitely armed. And I'm pretty sure they were elves. I mean, yeah, they had glamours, but I know an elf when I see one."

Hawk saw a few more people before he finally leapt from the oh-so-comfortable leather chair and leaned into the assistant manager's office, where Dru was talking to an elderly human woman.

"Why yes," the woman was saying, "I do believe that they were gnomes. It's the only thing that makes sense. Although I think the sixth one was an elf."

"Thanks, ma'am, you can go." Then Dru looked up at Hawk. "You need something?"

"To be talkin' to you for a sec."

"Sure."

The woman walked out of the office and Hawk walked in.

"Whaddaya think?" Dru asked.

"I think we need to be gettin' Boneen's bony ass in here."

"Yeah." Dru shook his head. "How many people you got?"

"Three to six."

"Oh, I got up to fifteen—and one guy who says the bank wasn't robbed. He was my favorite."

"Great." Hawk motioned for his partner to get up. "C'mon, let's get Martel to inventory what was stolen and see what we can do about gettin' the peel-back as soon as possible."

"Sure." Dru grinned. "But you still owe me a copper."

FOUR

TORIN AND DANTHRES RETURNED TO THE CASTLE AND IMMEDIATELY sent two guards to the shop to bring Elthor's body. They then retired to the squadroom, each of them sitting at their desk until the guards returned.

Fanthral stayed with them in the squadroom, to Torin's annoyance. He was concerned that the elf was going to dog their every step during the investigation. The erstwhile general was now standing near the pegboard, arms folded over his chest.

Torin couldn't even hope that Fanthral would be distracted by someone else, as the three of them were alone in the squadroom. Osric wasn't in his office, Dru and Hawk were on the bank robbery case, and Iaian and Grovis weren't at their desks, either.

"Where will the body be stored once those guards bring him back?" Fanthral asked.

"That's actually a good question," Danthres said, sounding surprised to be saying such a thing about Fanthral. "Without Boneen to put the bodies in stasis . . ."

Torin frowned. That was a problem, as Boneen's magic was all that kept the corpses from decaying prematurely.

Sergeant Jonas picked that moment to zip in, his green cloak billowing behind him as he placed parchments on both Iaian's and Grovis's desks. "Not to worry—Dru and Hawk had a similar issue during the Corvin case. Boneen set up a sprite to take care of that until he got back."

"Oh. Joy." Danthres let out a sigh as Jonas dashed back out of the room. "Bad enough we'll have to deal with that damned gryphon, now we get one of his sprites on top of it?"

Fanthral folded his arms and then smiled. "You object to sprites, do you, halfbreed?"

"I object to magic," Danthres said pointedly. "It never fails to give me a headache, and always has since I first left home."

Blinking, Fanthral parroted Danthres's words. "'Left home'? You were not born in Cliff's End?"

Raising an eyebrow, Danthres said, "Not that it's any of your business, but no, I wasn't."

"Interesting. That means you must have been born in Sorlin."

"Yes, what of it?" Danthres asked defensively.

"In that case, you must be quite displeased."

Now Danthres rose from her chair. "What, precisely, do I have to be displeased about? I have nothing against Sorlin, it is one of the few places where those of my kind can—"

"It *was*." Fanthral's interruption was in an uncharacteristically quiet tone. "The council disbanded about two months ago."

Danthres's face fell. "That's not possible."

Torin also got up. "How do you know this?"

Through clenched teeth, Danthres said, "He can't *possibly* know this. All proper elves stay away from Sorlin. It's an abomination. If you don't ask me, ask *any elf*!" She now walked up to Fanthral, jabbing a finger into his chest. "I will not listen to you tell falsehoods about my home."

"They're not falsehoods, Lieutenant." Fanthral, Torin noted, was now referring to her respectfully by rank rather than by the "halfbreed" term of derision. "I was in Sorlin before I came here. You see, lothSerra isn't the only former elf lord I've been chasing. He is, in fact, the last of three. The gem led me to the first two in Sorlin, but by the time I arrived, they had both died of natural causes."

Torin snorted. "I can't imagine former elven nobility would be welcome in Sorlin."

"Then you'd be wrong," Danthres snapped. "The council's policy is to allow anybody to come live there if they so desired, as long as they were not disruptive. If the elves he was chasing went there, they would be granted safe entry and be permitted to stay as long as they wished."

That surprised Torin—but then, Danthres hadn't been very forthcoming with details about her childhood in that southern land, and Torin had never met anyone else from there in his wanderings.

Were Fanthral not present, Torin would have asked her what exactly she did to get herself kicked out of there, if they were so accommodating to all and sundry.

Then again, if anybody could be disruptive, it was Danthres . . .

"What happened?" Danthres asked.

Fanthral frowned. "I beg your pardon?"

"You said you were in Sorlin two months ago when the council disbanded. I ask you again: What *happened*?"

"I was not told the specifics," Fanthral finally said. "However, their population has been falling below subsistence levels of late, plus the past few years have been bad for crops."

Torin nodded. He knew that the southern lands had had less than the usual amount of rainfall these past few years, and that had had a deleterious effect on their crop yields.

"Many have returned to the elven lands since the Elf Queen's fall," Fanthral continued, "others have travelled elsewhere. The stigma of being a free thinker has lessened all across Flingaria, and the need for a refuge has similarly decreased. So many departed that they felt they were no longer viable as a community."

Danthres held up a hand. "Wait, some went back to live among the elves? Sorlin was formed by people who were exiled—"

"By the Elf Queen," Fanthral said insistently. "Her policies are no longer in place, and the Consortium has officially welcomed all full-blooded elves and their families to come home."

That elicited a snort from Danthres. "Of course, only the pure-breds may come home."

However, Torin noted the entire phrase. "You said 'and their families.'"

"Yes." Fanthral now looked distinctively uncomfortable. "Those who mated with outsiders were permitted to come home as well—along with any offspring they might have produced."

"How generous," Danthres said tartly.

"It *was* generous, halfbreed." Fanthral's brief bout with politeness had apparently ended. "To allow such filth to pollute our homeland—"

"I take it, General," Torin said quickly, "that you were against this edict?"

"Of course I was!" Fanthral spoke as if any other answer was absurd—which, to a full-blooded elf of noble birth, it was.

Before Danthres could respond tartly to that—Torin knew that look on her face, and things would come to blows after a couple more exchanges—Jonas mercifully came back into the squadroom.

"Lieutenants, Abrik and Bonce are back with a dead body. They're waiting by the staircase."

"Good." Torin immediately headed toward the exit.

Fanthral moved to do likewise, but Danthres blocked his way. "This conversation will be continued at a later date."

"There is nothing more to say, Lieutenant. Your home is no more. If it means so much to you, why did you leave?" Then he gave that mirthless smile again, which Torin was already learning to despise. "But, as you say, we will continue this conversation later."

Danthres scowled at Fanthral before they all went out into the hallway and toward the back, to the narrow, winding staircase that took one to Boneen's lair in the basement. Abrik and Bonce were standing at the top of the stairs, the former holding the corpse by the ankles, the latter from under the shoulders.

"We ain't actually, y'know, goin' down there, like?" Abrik asked.

"I'm afraid so," Torin replied with a smile. "Don't worry, Boneen isn't there."

Bonce shuddered. "That's what worries me. If he *is* down there, I know what's gonna happen: he bitches at me for invading his space and makes me leave as fast as possible. I don't *mind* that. I'm *used* to that."

Fanthral regarded Torin. "A disagreeable sort, this Boneen?"

"On a good day, he's disagreeable. Regardless, we'll be fine. Come."

Danthres had grabbed a couple of torches and handed one to Torin, who led the way down. His partner waited until Fanthral and the two guards went ahead before bringing up the rear. This way they would have maximum light.

Torin also knew that she let him go first so *he* would have to deal with the gryphon.

The group went down the winding staircase, Torin pulling his cloak of office around himself as it grew colder.

"Your mage doesn't light the staircase?" Fanthral asked testily.

Torin shrugged. "He generally only enters via a Teleport Spell, and he does not encourage others to enter at all."

At the bottom, Torin was greeted by the massive wooden door. There was no other access to the landing save for the staircase behind him. The door's ornate knocker matched that of the gryphon image etched on the chest of Torin's leather armor.

The moment his boots hit the floor of the landing, the gryphon's beak started to move, and a squeaky voice came from it.

"What do you want?"

Fanthral jumped behind Torin, which gave him a certain amused satisfaction. "We need to deposit a body in Boneen's laboratory."

"Who are you?"

"Lieutenant Torin ban Wyvald, with Lieutenant Danthres Tresyllione and Guards Abrik and Bonce."

"What case?"

"The death of Elthor lothSerra."

A lengthy pause followed.

Torin looked back at Fanthral. "Sergeant Jonas should have already filed the initial paperwork for the case with Ep. If so, the gryphon will let us in."

"Ep?" Fanthral asked.

"The imp that manages our files."

A click then sounded form the door, with the squeaky voice saying, "You may bring the body inside. The sprite will give you instructions. If you touch anything that you are not specifically instructed by the sprite to touch, be aware that neither I nor my caster will be responsible for the consequences."

The gryphon beak stopped moving, and Torin pushed the large door inward.

Entering behind him, Fanthral said, "I see what you mean by disagreeable."

"You have no idea." Torin put out his torch, as the windowless room was lit by what he assumed to be a magickal source. Several tables held bodies that were glowing with the blue tinge of a Preservation Spell, and there were shelves covered with parchments and various other objects, including a large number of jars labeled in a language Torin couldn't read, but knew to be the written language created by the Brotherhood of Wizards. Only mages could read the words in that script.

Abrik and Bonce brought the body in, with Danthres coming up behind them. "Lord and Lady, I hate coming down here. The smell alone . . ."

Fanthral's nose was wrinkling, and Torin found himself grateful that he didn't have the sensitive nose of an elf—or a half-elf. "Is that—goblin dung?"

"We've never had the courage to ask," Torin said. "However—"

Before he could complete his thought, there was a brief flash of light, and then a small, green, winged female creature appeared. She had abnormally wide eyes for her size, no obvious nose, and a tiny mouth. She flew around the room with a tiny buzzing noise, finally alighting on one of the empty tables.

"Body place will you table on this."

Abrik and Bonce looked at each other, shrugged, and then placed the body on the table. The sprite lifted off just before they did so.

Then the sprite flew around the body seven times. When she was done, Elthor had the same blue tinge as the other corpses in the room. Another flash of light, and the sprite was gone.

"That," Danthres said, "will keep the body preserved until Boneen deigns to once again grace us with his presence."

"Very well." Fanthral nodded and clapped his hands. "Now, from what Osric told me, your procedure is to examine the place where the crime occurred, yes?"

"No," Danthres snapped.

Torin winced. "Well, yes, actually, that is *technically* our procedure, but without our M.E., there is little that can be done—"

"Are you saying that you can do nothing without the help of this mage?" Fanthral asked archly.

Regarding the elf coolly, Torin said, "If you would let me finish, sir—there is little that can be done so many days after the event."

Danthres added, "Haven's Way is a well-trodden thoroughfare. If we can arrive at the scene at a time close to when it happened, then there might be evidence that can aid us in catching the perpetrator. But outdoor scenes are impossible under the best of circumstances, and these are far from that. Boneen's peel-back is truly all that will be of use to us at this late date."

Again, Fanthral folded his arms. "Captain Osric told me that you two were his best investigators. He went on at some length on the subject. Indeed, he informed me that it was the two of you who caught the man who killed Olthar lothSirhans. He informed me of this when he assigned me to you. That means that you will do as I say—as a courtesy to a visiting dignitary."

Danthres rolled her eyes. "'Dignitary'? That's what you call yourself?"

"It's what the Consortium calls me, and what Lord Albin and Lady Meerka call me. If you have an issue with my instructions—"

Torin deliberately stepped between Danthres and Fanthral. Across the room, Abrik and Bonce were exchanging nervous glances, looking like they wanted to be anywhere but here.

"There is," Torin said, "no need to bring the Lord and Lady into this. If you wish us to investigate Haven's Way, then, by all means, we shall investigate it."

"Excellent. Let us proceed."

With that, Fanthral stormed out of Boneen's lair. Torin heard his boots clomping on the winding stairs going back up.

Bonce and Abrik hurried after the elf, seeing his exit as the excuse they needed to get the hell out.

Danthres just looked at Torin, who pointed an accusatory finger at his partner. "Do *not* look upon me as if this is *my* fault, Danthres. You've annoyed far too many members of the court as it is. Sooner or later, you're going to annoy the wrong one—or worse, the Lord and Lady themselves."

"Oh, I know this isn't *your* fault, Torin." She smiled. "Nice rant, though."

"Thank you," Torin said dryly.

"No, I blame my father's people for producing such a perfect ass as Fanthral. Come, let us waste our time on Haven's Way and get that much further from finding the truth."

"What's to find?" Torin left Boneen's lair, waiting for Danthres to come out behind him so he could close the door. Upon doing so, the lock made a clicking sound. "LothSerra died of an overdose of Bliss. The rest of this is wishful thinking on Fanthral's part. We simply require Boneen to return to verify this fact, and we can send the general on his merry way."

Danthres gave Torin a smile. "All right, I know why *I* dislike the shitbrain so much—what do *you* have against him?"

As they ambled up the winding staircase, Torin provided Danthres with a brief précis of his encounters with then-General Fanthral during the war.

Whatever comment Danthres may have made was swallowed by their being once again in the elf's presence. "Shall we proceed?" Fanthral asked.

"Of course," Torin said, glad that it was, at least, a nice fall day outside. The walk to Goblin Precinct would be a pleasant one.

At least until they made it clear to Fanthral that nothing there was of value.

FIVE

BONEEN ARRIVED AT THE CASTLE AND NEARLY COLLAPSED.

Reaching out, he steadied himself against one of the castle's stone walls and tried to get his breathing under control. There was a time, not that long ago, when Boneen could use a Teleport Spell to bring himself halfway across Flingaria and not even notice. But now, just a quick jaunt from Barlin to Cliff's End had him exhausted.

Looking around, he also realized that he hadn't materialized in his laboratory as he'd intended, but instead right above it in one of the corridors. Boneen sighed, wondering if this meant what he thought it did: he was getting too old to do Teleport Spells.

And that was the first step.

Of the everyday spells that wizards cast, Teleport was the most intensive and difficult. Lately, that meant that Boneen had to take a nap after casting it, though even when he didn't, he enjoyed a good nap. Naps were the backbone of productivity, in his mind. If you took a nap, you could then continue to function for hours on end.

And he obviously needed one now.

Feeling he could now stand upright on his own, he slowly let go of the wall. To his relief, he remained upright, his knees unbuckled, for seconds after abandoning the wall's support. This raised his spirits a bit, and he decided to go ahead and try walking.

He made it all the way to the end of the corridor when Osric turned the corner and said, "Finally, Boneen, you're back."

Holding up a hand, the magickal examiner said, "Whatever it is you need me to do, it shall have to wait. I have had a very trying day, and I need to rest."

Osric let loose with one of the scowls that he often employed in an attempt to intimidate his subordinates. "Your day is unlikely to have been as trying as mine."

Boneen smirked. "Obviously you've never dealt with the brotherhood's Ruling Committee. I have spent the entire time I've been away listening to endless tirades about responsibility and accountability—and that was after I spent the better part of a day repeating my own knowledge of Lord Ythran's mendacity, since I was unfortunate enough to be the one to report it to the brotherhood. And do remind me to strangle ban Wyvald and Tresyllione for sticking me in the middle of that idiocy."

"They didn't have a choice, Boneen."

"Of course they had a choice!" Boneen snapped. "They could have let Ythran and Sir Malik continue their ridiculous false church, and no one would have been the wiser."

"They were attempting to catch a murderer." Osric kept talking before Boneen could respond. "And that's of no consequence right now. Since you're back, I need you to perform a couple of peel-backs and examine a body."

Boneen stared at Osric. "Are you mad? After all that nonsense I just described, I had to teleport here from Barlin. Trust me, Captain, I will not be casting any Inanimate Residue Spells until *after* I've had my nap."

"Fine, then you can examine the body, at least. We need to be certain that he died of a Bliss overdose."

With a snarl, Boneen asked, "Since when do you concern yourself with overdoses? If some idiot takes more of a drug than he can handle, then the world's better off without them."

"I agree," Osric said slowly, "but in this case, the victim is Elthor lothSerra—a former favorite of the—"

"Yes, yes, I know who he is," Boneen snapped. He let out a short breath, then coughed, cursing himself for getting so old. "He's freshly dead in Cliff's End?"

Osric nodded. "You knew him?"

Boneen nodded. "When I was younger, I was part of a delegation to the Elf Queen's domain to petition to harvest some farmland. Certain herbs that we require for spellcasting grow best in the western lands. We spent the better part of a month there, discussing things with the Elf Queen and several of her advisors—including Elthor."

Then Osric frowned. "You said, 'freshly dead in Cliff's End.' That's an odd way of phrasing the question."

"Well spotted." Boneen shook his head. "I'm honestly surprised he survived the Elf Queen's ouster."

"He didn't survive it particularly well. He was found in Haven's Way, begging for scraps."

"And eventually took too much Bliss?" Boneen asked.

Again, Osric nodded. "That, at least, is the hypothesis. We need you to look over the body and verify that that is, in fact, how he died."

"Whose case is this?"

"Tresyllione and ban Wyvald."

"Good," Boneen said emphatically. "That means there's a chance it will come out well." He shuddered, realizing he'd actually said that aloud. "Please don't tell them I said that," he asked Osric in an almost pleading tone.

The captain actually smiled at that—and it was his real smile, the one he never showed anyone, though Boneen had seen it once or twice. "Worry not, Boneen, I will keep it secret that there is someone in Flingaria aside from yourself that you think well of."

"Thank you."

Osric's smile fell. "But there's another wrinkle."

Boneen raised an eyebrow. "Oh?"

"The lieutenants are assisting an elven emissary named Fanthral."

"I don't know him."

"Be grateful." Osric's scowl came back. "I fought against him during the war. I did manage to gain his respect, which is more than he managed with me."

Boneen snorted at that. Osric's respect was, he knew, not often given. Not as rarely as Boneen's respect, but still it was rare coin.

"Fanthral," Osric explained, "came to Cliff's End to bring Elthor back to the Consortium for war trials. His being dead is a bit of a nuisance."

Putting his head in his hands, Boneen muttered, "War trials? Really?"

"You object to war trials?"

"I do not see the point." Boneen sighed. "The Elf Queen is dead. People need to get on with their lives and not dwell so much on the past. That way lies madness, believe you me." Another sigh. "Very well, I will somehow find it within myself to examine Elthor's body."

"What about the peel-back? The scene is already several days old, so you're our only likely source of anything useful from there."

Boneen moved past Osric toward the staircase, ignoring the question. He wanted to get to Elthor's body so he could get a nap.

Osric bellowed, "Boneen!" That made the M.E. stop in his tracks.

He turned around. "What?"

"Will you be able to perform the peel-back on Haven's Way?"

Realizing the captain was not going to give this up without an answer, Boneen simply said, "Perhaps. Allow me to perform the examination, first."

"When the brotherhood provided you, Boneen," Osric said, "it was under the provision that you perform the duties required of the position. Given what you just went through, I can't imagine your being too terribly happy with me reporting to Gunderson that you have not been fulfilling your duties, nor to Fanthral that our magickal examiner impeded an investigation important to the Consortium."

Boneen glowered at Osric. Lord Ythran's replacement, Gunderson was a humorless old bastard—even by the high standards of the brotherhood's ability to churn out such. Indeed, Boneen had always considered himself a past master of the breed.

However, he wasn't about to give up. "You cannot possibly

imagine, Captain, that anyone in the brotherhood finds the changeable politics of mortals to be anything other than boring. I am here as a courtesy. I can assure you that the brotherhood takes no interest in the wishes of either the Consortium or of Lord Albin and Lady Meerka."

Osric bared his teeth in what could charitably be named a smile. "We'll leave aside the hilarity of your dismissing the two people who provide you with shelter, a laboratory, and the freedom to do as you wish when you're not on duty. The question, Boneen, is which tedium do you prefer less—doing as I ask, or listening to Gunderson drone on about the responsibilities of your office?"

For several seconds, Boneen was silent.

"Well?" Osric prompted.

"I'm thinking it over," Boneen said sourly. "Very well, I will examine the body, and then eventually I will go to Haven's Way." He carefully did not commit to a specific time frame.

"Good."

Then Boneen's curiosity got the better of him. "You mentioned two peel-backs."

"I did, yes. The other is for the Cliff's End Bank's main branch. It was robbed. Dru and Hawk are handling that, and it happened this morning and has actual witnesses, so we'll muddle through without you."

"Good to know."

Osric turned on his heel and walked toward the east wing where his office lay.

Boneen trudged down the winding staircase, muttering to himself. "'Freedom to do as I wish.' If I had *that* freedom, I damn well wouldn't be *here*, would I?" He grumbled as he got to the landing and opened the door with a gesture.

Ilya, his sprite, appeared upon his entrance. "Home to you welcome are!"

"Oh, do *stop* that," Boneen said with a roll of his eyes. "Speak Common, if you please. You're not fooling anyone with that attempt to sound exotic."

The sprite pouted as she flew around the room. "But it's *fun!*"

"Only for you."

"Who else matters?"

"I do, or have you forgotten who saved you from Gunderson?"

At that, Ilya shuddered. Ilya had belonged to Lord Ythran, and when he was removed from his station, all his belongings went to his replacement. However, Gunderson had long had an aversion to sprites, and he was going to destroy her until Boneen intervened. "I'm sorry, truly. How was your trip?"

The M.E. said nothing at first, choosing instead to gaze around the lab—both visually and magickally. Nothing seemed to be missing, and the only addition was the body of an elf on one of the tables.

"There were intruders while I was gone?"

"Only twice. Lieutenants Dru and Hawk came in looking for something—they didn't say what, only that it related to the Corvin case."

Boneen waved a dismissive hand. "Dru and Hawk are already on another case, so that one must be closed, and therefore irrelevant. What was the other intrusion?"

"This morning. Lieutenants ban Wyvald and Tresyllione, along with two guards and an elf I didn't recognize."

Walking over to the elven corpse, Boneen nodded. "That would be that Fanthral person that Osric so dislikes." He stared down at the body. It took him a bit to recognize Elthor lothSerra. "What a waste."

"What is?"

Pointing at the corpse, Boneen said, "Him. He was part of the Elf Queen's court, a vibrant, powerful man. To see him reduced to this . . ." He put a hand to his forehead and rubbed it. Annoyance at Osric had put the fatigue aside for a bit, but it was coming back again. "Find me a stool, will you please?"

"Of course." Ilya flew over to a stool that was buried under some parchments. She used her wings to fan the parchments onto the floor, then picked the stool up and brought it over.

Boneen gave a glower at least as nasty as the one he gave Osric. "You do realize I'm going to make you clean that up, yes?"

Ilya looked abashed. "I'm sorry."

"You may apologize all you wish," Boneen said as he clambered onto the stool, relieved to be off his feet, "but you will still have to clean it up."

"Feh."

She flew off, and Boneen ignored her. Something didn't sit right with him. Elthor never partook of any illicit substances. He never drank, never sniffed, never smoked. All the times Boneen spent in the elf's company, he never evinced any interest in artificial stimulation of any kind.

Yet here he was overdosing. *Was he that miserable?*

"Stupid question," he muttered. "He lost everything, in a manner that was depressingly permanent, and wound up begging in Goblin Precinct."

Ilya flitted by. "Did you say something?"

Swatting at her like she was a fly, Boneen said, "No, I'm simply talking to myself. It's my only guarantee of intelligent conversation."

Again Ilya said, "Feh," and flew off.

Reaching into his pouch, Boneen pulled out a root. Snapping it in two, it let out a bitter scent into the air. Boneen then muttered an incantation.

Expecting to find impressions of the drug in his system, instead Boneen felt a tug at his mind. Anticipating only a simple narcotic, he found something much greater.

Quickly, he muttered another incantation, causing a mage bird to appear before him. "Find Lieutenants ban Wyvald and Tresyllione and inform them that they must return to the castle immediately. It's about Elthor lothSerra here. They should be somewhere between here and Haven's Way. Go." The glowing white bird flew away soundlessly.

If he had the wherewithal, Boneen would have teleported to Haven's Way and brought the detectives back here right away. But it was just as well that he had nowhere near the will to do so. Leaving aside any other considerations, Tresyllione always threw up when she was teleported, and he was going to have a hard enough time getting Ilya to clean up the parchments as it was. Asking her to clean Tresyllione's vomit would probably be her breaking point.

Speaking of whom, Ilya flitted over to hover near Boneen's nose. "What is it, Boneen, what's wrong?"

"Quite a bit, I'm afraid. Elthor's death has far more ramifications than we originally thought."

SIX

OSRIC HAD ALMOST MADE IT TO HIS OFFICE WHEN THE PAGEBOY CAME by with orders to take the captain to see Lord Albin. With a sigh, Osric followed the young man through the corridors of the castle's western wing. While meetings with the head of the demesne used to be fairly regular when Osric first took on the job of Captain of the Castle Guard, after a few years, Albin learned to trust Osric's judgment and didn't feel the need for regular updates.

The downside of that was when Osric *was* summoned, it was almost always because of a serious problem. Most often it was due to a case being political in nature, which meant a great deal of scrutiny for him and his detectives. The last time, it was during the Cynnis case, when Osric had to talk Arra Cynnis's father out of requesting that the captain fire Tresyllione and ban Wyvald.

Thinking back on it, Osric realized that most of the difficult meetings he had with the lord of the demesne were cases he'd given to his two best detectives—often involving Tresyllione pissing someone off. It was the captain's considered opinion that, if he hadn't paired her up with the more affable ban Wyvald, he would've been forced to fire her years ago.

Which would have been unfortunate, since the pair of them truly excelled in the job. The Castle Guard had fulfilled Lord Albin's mandate swimmingly mainly due to the detective squad's success rate, and that rate was almost entirely on the backs of those two.

Upon entering the huge wooden double doors at the end of one corridor, Osric got a tight feeling in his stomach at the sound of Lord Albin sneezing.

It was unnecessary, of course. The first chill that signaled autumn's impending arrival was generally accompanied by Lord Albin getting the sniffles.

But during the first meeting Osric ever had with Lord Albin, eleven years ago, Albin was pale, sickly, sneezing, and constantly blowing his nose into an embroidered handkerchief.

Osric recalled the day quite clearly. The war had been over for half a year, and Osric had found himself adrift. He wound up—as did so many others—at Cliff's End on a chilly late-summer day. Citing his position as a former general in the service of King Marcus and Queen Marta, he requested an audience with Lord Albin, never for a moment expecting it to be granted.

When the pageboy arrived at the Dog and Duck Inn with the message that the Lord and Lady requested his presence at their dinner table, but first he was to meet with Lord Albin in his sitting room for drinks, Osric nearly fell over from the shock.

A fire was roaring in the fireplace on the left-hand side of the room, while Lord Albin—who had a monk's fringe of hair back then, and no mustache—sat on the couch, sneezing. "Ah, you must be General Osric! Please, do come in! Have a seat. Elron, please fetch the general a drink."

Osric hadn't even noticed the servant until Albin spoke to him. The servant—who had since died—moved silently through the room. He poured an amber liquid into a crystal glass and word-lessly handed it to Osric.

"Thank you," Osric said. Elron simply bowed in reply.

"That will be all, Elron," Albin said, and the servant shimmered out of the sitting room, closing the double doors. The creak of the wood was the only noise he made.

After sitting in a plush chair that was perpendicular to the couch, Osric said, "I have to admit, my Lord, to being surprised by your invitation."

"Really? You were the one who requested it."

"Yes, sir, but you were the one who granted it."

Albin laughed. "Well, why wouldn't I? Your record speaks for itself, and Sir Palrik speaks very highly of you."

Osric blinked. "'Sir' Palrik?" He had known Palrik as a particularly unimaginative officer.

"Yes, he's been a member of my court since birth. Insisted on enlisting in the army when the war started, though. Apparently had some kind of animus against the—" He cut himself off for a sneeze that shook the glass on the drinks cabinet. "Sorry. Against the Elf Queen. In any event, he spoke very highly of you."

"I'm grateful to hear that."

Albin laughed again, but this time it modulated into a cough that Osric sat uncomfortably through. "My apologies," Albin said, after getting his breathing under control. "I was simply amused that you did not return the compliment to Sir Palrik. That's good—you don't engage in insincere flattery. It isn't something I'd look for in a dinner companion, normally." He blew his nose again. "So, General Osric, what brings you to Cliff's End?"

"Well, for starters, my Lord, I'm no longer properly referred to with that rank. My term has ended. As for what brings me to Cliff's End—I am hopeful that I might find employment here. Perhaps sign on to a ship at the docks."

Tilting his head in surprise, Albin said, "I wasn't aware you had any naval experience."

Reluctantly, Osric said, "I don't."

"The best you could hope for would be to serve as a simple sailor. Surely a person with your experience can find something more—more lucrative?"

"Unlikely. I'm a soldier, my Lord, and there are no more wars to fight."

"But surely the army provided you with a pension?"

Osric smiled bitterly. "Surely you would think that, my Lord, but I'm afraid not. We were told that, when soldiers died, the money put aside for their pension was put back into the war effort. What we were not told was that that was the case for *all* the pension money, whether the soldier entitled to it was dead or alive. Which came as rather a shock to those of us fortunate enough to survive the war, only to find ourselves without what we were promised."

That prompted a frown. "Oh dear."

"I must confess, my Lord, that I used harsher language."

"No doubt." Albin sipped his drink.

"In any event, the last of my savings provided me with a week's lodgings at the Dog and Duck. I have that long to find employment, which may prove impossible. There is peace in Flingaria, my Lord, and that reduces the opportunities for making a living for those of us whose skills are best suited to war. Besides which, as you can see—" He pointed at the patch that covered his left eye, which back then was a cheap cloth one. "—those skills are now diminished."

"Ah, see, that's where—" Albin sneezed. "Excuse me. That's where you're wrong, General. Sorry, Osric. You see, there *is* still war. It's constantly being waged here in Cliff's End."

Osric frowned. He had heard of no conflict between Cliff's End and any of the other city-states.

"I speak metaphorically—but only barely." That was followed by yet another coughing fit. "My apologies. As I was saying, there is a war—against lawlessness and chaos. Cliff's End has long been a crossroads, with a population that increases every year—and with it comes a more entrenched criminal element. Many years ago, I expanded the mandate of the Castle Guard to maintain law and order within the city-state."

Nodding, Osric took a sip of his drink. He had heard a rumor to that effect, but he hadn't given it much thought.

"At present, the captain in charge is a man named Brisban, but he's dying. The physicians tell me he is unlikely to live out the week—and even if he recovers, he will no longer have a job. He has been a poor captain, and I need someone of superior intellect and experience." Albin smiled. "And then you fell into my lap."

That was followed by yet another coughing fit.

Osric accepted the offer eventually, of course, but it took him a few days to do so. For starters, he wasn't sure if he was truly as qualified as Albin thought. And given how ill he was during the meeting, Osric wasn't sure that Albin would necessarily outlive this Brisban person. He was worse during dinner, which he barely touched and during which he coughed and sneezed more than Osric thought possible in one sitting.

But then Brisban died and Albin got better, and Osric found no other job that wasn't menial, and decided it was worth a try. It helped that Albin offered him a salary that was twice what he'd made as a general. One of the first things he bought with his initial wages was a new silk eyepatch.

Now, Albin was sitting in a large chair next to the fireplace, which had a roaring fire going. Despite his proximity to the flames, he had a sweater wrapped tightly about his shoulders, and he was obviously shivering. These days, his hair was entirely gone, and he had let his mustache thicken to the point where it dominated his face, obscuring his mouth and the lower part of his nose. It also looked, rather revoltingly, as if it had caught quite a bit of the lord's mucus.

"Ah, Osric, come in!"

"My Lord." This time, since Albin was in the chair, and had moved it proximate to the fireplace, Osric took the couch.

"I need reassurances, Captain, that Fanthral is receiving every courtesy. It is critical that we maintain strong relations with the Consortium."

This allowed Osric to ask a question that had been preying on his mind ever since Fanthral showed up in Cliff's End. "Why?"

Albin had sneezed as he asked that, so he asked, "I beg your pardon?"

"Why is it so critical that we maintain strong relations with the Consortium? I hadn't even *heard* of the Consortium until Fanthral arrived."

"Between you and me, Captain—I haven't the faintest idea."

Osric's eyes widened. "Pardon me, my Lord?"

"All I *do* know is that I received a mage bird from the king and queen themselves, informing me that, for whatever reason, this latest provisional elven government is one we must maintain strong ties with." He shook his head and shivered some more. "A dozen years since the Elf Queen fell, and they've gone through at least three different governments, all of which have collapsed under the weight of their own incompetence. I fail to see why this is the one we must fawn over."

For several seconds, Osric simply stared at Albin. The last time he'd been summoned to this sitting room, Albin had also been uncharacteristically tetchy. That time it was because he needed to play nice with Sir Malik Cynnis due to his needing the latter's money for a project. Of course, Sir Malik's later disgrace in the same scandal that brought down Lord Ythran probably didn't do anything to help that project, whatever it was, along.

Still, Albin was not usually one to be this snappish, and this now marked twice in two visits that he'd been so.

After a sneeze, Albin said, "Also, I've been receiving queries all morning from virtually everyone in Cliff's End who has the prefix 'Sir' asking about the bank robbery. I assume you put Harcort Grovis's son on it?"

"No."

Staring at Osric through what he now saw were very rheumy eyes, Albin asked, "Whyever not? He knows the bank better than anyone."

"Actually, he doesn't, as his father sent him to us instead of letting him work at the bank."

"Yes, but surely he would have picked up something along the way."

Osric sighed. "I doubt it, given how little he's picked up on being a detective. My Lord, Grovis is our worst detective. Besides, he's unlikely to be objective."

Albin sneezed again. "Excuse me. And of what value is that? Objectivity is not always a virtue."

"It is if, for example, the thieves were aided by someone who works for the bank. It could be someone Grovis knows, and someone—especially Grovis—is less likely to accuse someone he knows of committing a crime."

"Perhaps you're right, but I still believe that he can be of use advising . . ." He trailed off. "I assume it's Dru and Hawk, since you put Tresyllione and ban Wyvald with Fanthral?"

Osric nodded.

"Very well. I hope you're right, Osric. The robbery is making a lot of very important people very nervous." Albin punctuated his remark with a coughing fit.

"Of course." Osric finished his drink and rose. "If that'll be all, my Lord?"

"Hm? Oh, yes, of course, Osric." Albin waved the captain off.

Leaving the sitting room as fast as he could, Osric hoped he wouldn't be summoned to the sitting room again for at least another week, since past history suggested it would be that long before Albin was well again.

SEVEN

ONCE AGAIN, JORBIN'S WAY WAS QUIET, AND HOBART WAS NOT happy.

He puffed away at one of his Barlin cigars. It was midday, the time-chimes having just rung twelve, and usually that would mean that Jorbin's Way would be packed with potential customers pushing past each other trying to find just the right thing to buy from Hobart—or, if they insisted, from one of the other merchants.

Hobart generally made a good living on Jorbin's Way selling an assortment of dry goods. Everything he sold was something easily packed up and moved elsewhere. Hobart had no interest in paying the exorbitant prices charged by the Brotherhood of Wizards for storage of perishable items. Better to just stick with something he could put in a box.

Lately, however, the crowds had diminished. Jorbin's catered to Cliff's End's middle- and lower-classes, with goods that could be found at a cheaper price than places with full-on storefronts, who had to mark up in order to keep up with their rent. Besides, the merchants on Jorbin's often could get items that weren't entirely above-board—or which weren't marked up due to tariffs, thanks to not having actually paid them.

One of the latter items was an entire bolt of linen from Saptor Isle that Hobart had from a shipmaster whose cousin's family grew flax and wove it into linen on the island. Saptor linens were always softer and more comfortable than those from the mainland—the shipmaster in question said it had something to do with winds or sunlight or some such thing. Hobart didn't give a goblin's foot about the details. The flax farmer had a surplus of linen after his family sold to various merchants, and gave that surplus to his cousin the shipmaster, who sold them to Hobart at a rate that was considerably lower than what he'd pay on the open market, but which still gave the shipmaster a tidy profit on, well, nothing. Even with Hobart's own mark up, he sold the best linen in Flingaria for less than half of what every other merchant charged.

And that, right there, was the crux of his problem, right there in that bolt of Saptor linen that sat, unpurchased, on his stand on the eastern end of Jorbin's Way. In the past, every time he got a shipment of Saptor linen, it was gone by the end of the day.

Today, though, he'd only sold a few yards, and that was to a couple of tourists who were on their way to the docks for a sea voyage. His regulars were nowhere to be found.

Then he saw a sight that normally filled him with dread, but today suffused him with uncharacteristic joy: two Cloaks heading down the way.

Lieutenants Tresyllione and ban Wyvald were striding purposefully through Jorbin's toward Haven's Way (and why they'd be going to that shithole, Hobart had no idea). But if anybody could do anything about this scourge that had ravaged Jorbin's, it was those two.

Happy to have an outlet, and only a little concerned that things had gotten so bad that he viewed the arrival of two Cloaks with anything other than annoyance, Hobart put out his cigar and jumped up and down to get their attention. "Oi! Lieutenants!"

They were, he noticed, walking with an armor-wearing elf who seemed more than a little perturbed.

Tresyllione looked down on him with her usual disdain. "We don't have time for you, Hobart."

"Look, I just need a moment, all right?"

The elf asked, "Who is this imbecile?"

"Hobart," ban Wyvald said with a smile. "One of the merchants."

"I know the type." The elf's mouth twisted in disgust. "I would prefer we not dally with him, as we have work to do, and he'll have our money pouches before long."

Smiling in that way that made her even uglier, Tresyllione said, "See, Hobart? He's only just met you, and he already knows you!"

"Oh, real funny, Lieutenant. Look, I got information that might be'a use to ya."

"You expect us to believe that?" Tresyllione asked.

"Oh, I believe it," ban Wyvald said.

"Thank you, Lieutenant." Hobart inclined his head toward ban Wyvald. "Always knew you were the brains of the partnership."

Continuing as if Hobart hadn't spoken, the red-bearded Cloak went on: "What I don't believe is that he'll name a price for this information that we'll be willing to pay."

Hobart pointed an accusatory finger at ban Wyvald. "Ah, see, that's where you're wrong, Lieutenant. Y'see, I ain't chargin' you nothin' for this little piece'a info."

"And I say again, you expect us to believe that?"

Snarling at Tresyllione, Hobart said, "Look, this is good stuff, an' if you don't want it—"

The big elf turned to leave. "I see no reason to continue to listen to this."

Realizing he wasn't going to get anywhere if he didn't provide at least one detail, and seeing that ban Wyvald and Tresyllione were starting to move to join the elf, Hobart said, "It's about Bliss!"

Ban Wyvald stopped and whirled around. "What about Bliss?"

Tresyllione looked at her partner. "What difference does it make? He's not worth the time."

"Let's hear him out," ban Wyvald said. "What about Bliss?"

Hobart smiled. "Thank you, Lieutenant. I knew I could count on you to—"

"Get on with it, please, Hobart," ban Wyvald said sharply.

"Right. Well, first of all, the stuff's a menace, all right? You know that profits on Jorbin's are down since midsummer? It's all 'cause'a Bliss. People're buyin' Bliss and that ain't leavin' them with enough silver left to buy something nice for themselves or nothin' like that. I mean, truly, it's so a merchant can't make an honest living in this town no more."

Tresyllione smiled that damned smile again. "And how would you know that?"

"You gonna keep makin' jokes, or you gonna let me provide my information?"

"Thus far," ban Wyvald said, "you haven't provided any information, merely complained about how Bliss has affected your business."

"Which," Tresyllione added, "is not something that falls within the Castle Guard's purview. And even if it did, I wouldn't care. Unless, of course, you were the one selling it, in which case, I doubt you'd be this helpful. So kindly get to it."

Hobart had to admit that Tresyllione was right on that score, though he'd never admit it to her. If he had the Bliss concession, he'd be happier than a gnome with a stepstool. "Look, I'm just buildin' to it, okay? Settin' the stage so that you'll be understandin' the context and such-like."

Glancing at Tresyllione, ban Wyvald smiled. "He's a bard now, it seems."

"It ain't just me, okay?" Hobart held out a hand, taking in all the other merchants on Jorbin's—many of whom were staring at this tableau with open-mouthed stupefaction to see Hobart willingly talk to Cloaks, but that was a sign of how desperate times were. Also, the fact that they had the ability to look at Hobart rather than deal with the throngs of customers spoke volumes, he hoped, to the two Cloaks. "Every merchant on the way's feelin' it. Bliss's a damn scourge, is what it is."

Tresyllione rolled her eyes. "Hobart, Bliss isn't illegal, so unless—"

"Wait." That was the elf, who now pushed past the two Cloaks and gazed down upon Hobart. "Tell me, merchant—are you familiar with who is providing this drug to the citizenry?"

"Who cares?" Tresyllione asked.

Whirling on the Cloak, the elf said, "I do. LothSerra died of an overdose of this Bliss substance. Perhaps he was indeed a beggar on Haven's Way as you claim, but someone gave him this drug. If we find the creators of it, we may find out who killed him."

"Oh, Lord and Lady," Tresyllione said, "for the twelfth time, he killed *himself.*"

"That has not been proven to my satisfaction."

Hobart had no idea what the dynamic was between the half-elf and the full-blooded elf, but he had a feeling it had something to do with Tresyllione being her usual bitchy self.

Either way, he was going to take advantage. "You wanna know who's makin' Bliss, do you?"

The elf turned back to Hobart. "Yes. Tell me," he pulled a longsword out of a back scabbard with a metallic scratch, "or I will run you through where you stand."

"Oh, please," Tresyllione said with mock-enthusiasm, "don't tell him anything, Hobart. Then he'll kill you, and we can arrest him for murder. It would make my day."

"Wouldn't make mine," Hobart muttered. He reached into his jacket pocket and pulled out another cigar. He held it toward the elf. "Can I interest you in—"

He put the tip of the sword near Hobart's neck. "Tell me what you know."

Hobart was seriously starting to reconsider this entire notion of talking to the Cloaks. Then again, this shitbrain wasn't a Cloak. "All right, all right, just put the sword down, okay?"

Slowly, the elf lowered the sword, but did not re-sheathe it.

Rubbing his neck, Hobart said, "All right, look, I don't know who exactly the Bliss pusher is—"

Tresyllione threw up her hands. "I knew it. He doesn't know shit!"

"Wait a second!" Hobart cried quickly, trying to forestall the re-raising of the elf's sword. "Thing is, there's one fella's been spendin' way more gold than he used to. Matter of fact, he never even used t'*have* gold. Was strictly silver an' copper, he was. But lately, he's spendin' like he's the owner of the blessed bank."

"The name, please, Hobart."

"Kempog."

"Oh, please." Tresyllione rolled her eyes again.

Looking at her, the elf asked, "You know this Kempog?"

Ban Wyvald nodded. "He's a dwarf, and a small-time thug. Works as an enforcer and a runner for various criminals. As Hobart said, he's always been fairly low-level."

"An' that's what's so weird. He ain't usually the type to go 'round in silks an' the like. But he is now."

Ban Wyvald exchanged a look with Tresyllione. Hobart had seen the two of them do this before—it was like they communicated via Thought Spell.

"All right, we'll take a look at Kempog." Every word came out of Tresyllione's mouth as if she was forcing it out. "Even if he isn't the one dealing Bliss, if he's throwing gold around now, we should find out what's changed."

"Agreed," ban Wyvald said with a firm nod.

"Yes," the elf said, "but first we shall investigate Haven's Way to see if we can learn anything."

"We'll learn nothing," Tresyllione said tightly. "The scene is days old, and—"

Before Hobart could take pleasure in watching the elf and Tresyllione go at it again—if they kept it up, he was going to sell tickets—a glowing white bird appeared before them.

The glow expanded to the point that Hobart had to shield his eyes. From seemingly all around them came words in a high-pitched voice: "Boneen requests that you return to the castle immediately. It is regarding Elthor lothSerra's body."

The glow grew even brighter, and then dimmed to nothing. The mage bird was gone.

"Dunno why they can't be sendin' messengers like everyone else," Hobart muttered as he blinked the spots out of his eyes.

"Boneen's back, it seems," ban Wyvald said dryly.

"And he's examined the body," Tresyllione added. "Let's go."

The Cloaks started back the way they came. The elf muttered something in Ra-Telvish that Hobart didn't recognize—his facility for the elven tongue was poor at best, and he was out of practice—and then went after them.

Hobart lit his cigar, took a puff on it, feeling the pleasant aroma of the smoke enter his lungs. "You're welcome!" he called after the Cloaks. "Bloody ingrates."

He headed back to his stand, hoping that he might actually sell something today.

EIGHT

"HEY, BOY, YOU COMIN' IN, OR WHAT?"

"Hm?" Grovis looked up and around at Iaian's entreaty, and realized that he hadn't the foggiest idea where he was or what he was doing. He was too busy wondering what was going on at his father's bank, and wondering why he hadn't yet gotten a message from Daddy or from Dru and Hawk or from *somebody*.

He couldn't believe that anyone would do such a thing. The Cliff's End Bank was a sacred trust with the citizenry, and if that was violated, the entire system fell apart and people would be back to hiding their gold in their mattresses.

So worried had he been, he had completely forgotten that he and Iaian had a case. Shortly after Torin and Danthres and that elven general had left for the body shop, a member of the youth squad had come running in to tell them that there had been a murder in Goblin Precinct.

Iaian had been talking to the guard from Goblin who was at the series of hovels on Orphan's Lane where the murder took place, while Grovis was pacing up and down the lane wondering why in Ghandurha's name nobody had *told* him anything yet!

"You mind getting your ass in here?" Iaian spoke with even more testiness in his voice than usual. "Y'know, to solve a murder?"

Grovis shook his head. "Yes, yes, of course, my apologies, I'm a bit—a bit distracted, I'm afraid."

"Well, cut it out. We got work to do."

They went into the tiny hovel, where there was the body of a human on the floor, head at an odd angle to the rest of him.

Seated on a small crate, which was all the furniture the residents had, was a crying woman. Another guard from Goblin was standing near her.

Iaian looked down at the woman. "You the victim's wife?"

She shook her head. "Elko and me, we ain't, well, married, exactly."

Then Iaian turned to look at Grovis, who looked around, confused. "What?"

Chuckling, Iaian said, "Damn, two people living in sin, I thought for sure you'd make a remark. You really *are* off your game, ain'tcha?"

Grovis put his hands on his hips. "What is *that* supposed to mean?"

"Never mind." Iaian turned back to the woman. "Can you tell me what happened here?"

"Can tell you *exactly* what, well, happened. It was Brindy. He, well—all right, see, Brindy? He, well, he likes his Bliss. But after what happened with Jhef and Tiny, Urgoth wouldn't deal with him no more."

"Who's Urgoth?" Iaian asked.

"He's the dwarf. He deals the, well, Bliss 'round here. Y'know?"

"Okay, so Urgoth wouldn't deal to Elko?"

"No!" The woman shook her head. "Ain't you payin' attention? Urgoth wouldn't deal to *Brindy* 'cause'a what happened to, well, Jhef and Tiny. 'Specially Tiny. Tiny was always a pain in every-body's ass ever since Grunty left town."

Iaian held up his hands. "Okay, ma'am, I'm sorry, but—" He shook his head. "I need you to focus. What did Tiny do to Brindy?"

"Tiny didn't do nothin' to Brindy! But Brindy went and pissed off Urgoth, so Urgoth wouldn't give no Bliss to Brindy no more!"

Glancing over at Grovis, Iaian asked, "You gettin' all this, boy?"

Grovis blinked. He had been thinking about what Daddy must have been going through. The family had only just gotten over the double scandal of his cousin Cam hiring a sex-sim shortly before his fiancée Arra Cynnis was killed by a succubus. Well, actually, it was a hone-onna, but Grovis had given up correcting the rest of the family, who kept insisting it was a succubus, and after a while it just wasn't worth correcting. But adding this theft to the weight of what happened with Cam and Arra, it was just going to kill the family. Grovis had no idea what he was going to do.

Which meant he had no idea what Iaian was doing or talking about.

"I'm sorry?" he said lamely.

Now it was Iaian's turn to put his hands on his hips. "Oh for Wiate's sake, will you get your head in the game?"

"Of course, of course, I'm sorry. Now, then, madam, you say the victim is Brindy?"

The woman wiped a tear off with the back of her hand. "No, the guy who, well, killed the victim is Brindy. Elko."

Grovis frowned. "I'm sorry, was it Elko or Brindy?"

"C'mon, boy," Iaian said, "even *I* know that Elko's the victim." He turned to the woman. "So Brindy killed him because Urgoth told him to?"

"No! Dammit, ain't you payin' *any* attention?" The woman sighed. "Urgoth wouldn't give Brindy Bliss no more, so Elko, well, he said he'd get Brindy his Bliss for him, since Elko didn't take that stuff, and Brindy did. But then Urgoth got all, well, suspicious and stuff, because Elko, he said that he was, well, buyin' the Bliss for me, but I can't actually take Bliss. I mean, I tried once, but I was, well, allergic to it, got all puffy and such-like. So Urgoth, he found that out, and it didn't take long for him to figure out that Elko was doin' it for Brindy, and Urgoth was all pissed about what happened with Tiny and Jhef, so there was no way he was selling no more Bliss to Elko because he didn't want Brindy to get none, and Brindy got all pissed, and that was that. So you gonna arrest Brindy, or what?"

Unable to help himself, Grovis once again said, "I'm sorry. I'm afraid I lost track a bit—is Jhef the one who sold the Bliss to Urgoth, which forced him to kill Brindy?"

Iaian just stared at Grovis. "All right, that's it. Get your ass back to the castle."

"I'm s—"

Holding up a hand, Iaian said, "If you say 'I'm sorry' one more time, I'm gonna run you through with my sword. Your mind ain't on the case, and you're a crappy enough detective when you're payin' attention. You ain't worth shit to me like this. So go back to the castle and see if you can find out what happened to Daddy's bank. I'll take care'a this."

Grovis hesitated. "Are you sure? Regulations are that two detectives are supposed to deal with—"

Iaian rolled his eyes the way he seemed to at least twelve or thirteen times daily. "Please. We know who did it—just have to find Brindy and stick him in the hole. I think I can handle that. Get outta here."

At that moment, Grovis felt an emotion he'd never felt regarding his partner before. "Thank you," he said emphatically. He wasn't even too perturbed that Iaian had insulted him while letting him do what he preferred to do.

Without another word, he turned and left the hovel with its dead body and its annoying woman and her ridiculous story about people taking too much Bliss.

As he worked his way down Orphan's Lane back toward Meerka Way, the main thoroughfare of the city-state that would lead him back to the castle, he regretted his thoughts. Brindy—or was it Elko?—was a victim, someone whose life was unfairly taken from him.

And for what? For this ridiculous drug? Grovis had no comprehension, none, of why anyone would use a drug to substitute for happiness. Why, all one needed to do was find solace in Ghandurha and his noble teaching, and a happy life was guaranteed!

Although he didn't do anything quite so ridiculous as turn back, he did regret leaving Iaian with this case. Still, his partner was, in all likelihood, correct in that he could handle this alone. After all, he'd been in the Castle Guard for more than two decades—as he never tired of reminding Grovis—so surely he could handle a simple dispute-turned-murder.

When he reached the tree-lined pathway to the castle entrance, Grovis saw the familiar Cloaks of Dru and Hawk. In truth, what he recognized were Hawk's dreadlocks, which extended down past the gryphon emblem on his cloak.

"Ahoy, Dru! Hawk!"

The lieutenants stopped walking and turned around. "Oh, hey, Grovis," Dru said unenthusiastically.

"So, what news?" Grovis asked as he jogged to catch up with the pair of them. "Are you close to finding the malefactors who have soiled my family name?"

Dru and Hawk exchanged quick glances. "Er, well, we ain't got nothin' yet," Hawk finally said. "Witnesses weren't all that helpful, and far as we can tell, the robbers used glamours, so can't nobody identify them."

"What about the security?"

Again, Dru and Hawk exchanged glances. "What security?" Dru asked.

Grovis stared open-mouthed at the detectives. "Didn't Than tell you about the security?"

Dru grunted. "All Mr. Martel told us was how worried your Daddy was gonna be."

"Yeah, when he wasn't bitchin' that we wasn't bringin' the M.E. along."

"And hey," Dru said with a sudden smile, inexplicably slapping Grovis on the back, "why didn't you tell us about your dad?"

Grovis blinked. "I'm sorry?" He was saying that far too often today.

"Martel told us about the big news!"

Now Grovis was completely confused. "Dru, what in Ghandurha's name are you *talking* about?"

"Your dad," Hawk said slowly, "gettin' on the rolls."

His eyes widening, Grovis said, "What!? Daddy's going to be on the rolls?"

Dru swallowed, suddenly seeming nervous. "Well, that's what Martel said. I mean, he coulda been—"

"That's amazing! Oh, that's *wonderful*, that the Lord and Lady think highly enough of Daddy that—" He cut himself off. "Hang on—you said Than told you this?"

Hawk nodded.

"I don't believe it. Why would he tell Than and not me?"

The three of them entered the castle. Grovis was devastated. His father had been wanting to become a member of the Lord and Lady's court since he was a teenager. Their family had always had money, but not the full-on success that led to a title.

But when the Hazlars had their falling out with Lady Meerka and left Cliff's End, allowing the Cliff's End Bank to merge with the Hazlar Bank, Daddy had thought that it would be the step that would enable him to finally become Sir Harcort.

However, that did not explain why Daddy didn't say anything to his youngest son about it.

Upon entering the east wing, they saw Osric coming from the other side of the castle. He fixed his one-eyed gaze directly on Grovis. "What are *you* doing here?"

"Iaian instructed me to return to the castle, as he felt that my expertise was better suited to assisting the lieutenants here with their case."

Osric snarled. "More likely he got tired of you being so distracted over Daddy's bank. This is why I *didn't* want you on the case."

"Actually," Dru said, "we can use him. Turns out there's a security system in the bank that the robbers worked around. Only reason we even know about it's Grovis—bank manager never mentioned it"

Leading the detectives into the squadroom, Osric asked, "What kind of security system?"

"Good question." Hawk stared at Grovis.

Putting his annoyance at Daddy's lack of communication aside, Grovis said, "It's a theft deterrent from the Brotherhood of Wizards. All money deposited inside the bank is charmed, and when it's withdrawn, the charm is removed. If the charm isn't removed properly, the coins all become coated with a red shell that makes them worthless."

Sergeant Jonas came dashing out of the kitchen area, shuffling parchments as usual.

"Jonas," Osric said, "have there been reports of anyone trying to pass red coins?"

Shaking his head, the sergeant said, "Not that I've heard, but I can put the word out to the precincts to be on the lookout."

"Do that." Osric rubbed the ever-present stubble on his cheeks. "Knowing this sooner would have helped."

"I think we oughtta be goin' back," Hawk said, "with Grovis this time, an' find out why he wasn't mentionin' the security."

Osric muttered something under his breath. "Oh, all right, since it's obvious that Grovis is even more useless to me than usual."

Before Grovis could defend himself against that slander, one of the youth squad came dashing in. Grovis had always been dubious about the notion of relying so heavily upon children to deliver messages, but he had to admit that it was a system that seemed to work. He wished, though, that Lady Meerka—who handled the finances for the demesne—would approve simply putting them on salary instead of forcing the employees of the Castle Guard to use their own hard-earned money to tip them.

This was a freckle-faced girl wearing a dress that looked as if it had been passed down to her through at least six generations. "There's been another robbery! The bank!"

"Don't be ridiculous, girl," Grovis said, "the bank has already been robbed once today."

"Naw," she said, "not the main branch, the one on Axe Lane!"

Grovis's heart started to pound in his chest. "I don't believe it! First Cam and Arra, now this!"

Dru looked at Hawk. "There's, what, two branches of the bank?"

"Three," Grovis said, "plus the main one."

"That's half your father's banks hit in one day." Osric let out a sigh. "Fine, all three of you go, and find out if the security system actually works."

"You got it, Cap'n," Dru said. "C'mon, Grovis, let's go rescue Sir Daddy's bank."

Shooting Dru a nasty look, Grovis followed him and Hawk back out of the castle once again. Daddy wasn't going to be "Sir" Anything if this kept up.

NINE

TORIN RUBBED HIS TEMPLES WITH THE TIPS OF HIS FINGERS AS HE strode past Fanthral and Danthres, hoping that he could perhaps get far enough ahead of them as they went up Meerka Way that he would be spared their tiresome arguing.

Unfortunately, it was not to be. Both his partner and the erstwhile general had the characteristic great height and long legs of the elven race, and that meant they could easily pace Torin and his shorter legs.

So he was subjected to the pair of them going at it for the better part of an hour.

It wouldn't have been so bad if it was Danthres's usual sniping. After a decade, Torin was well used to that.

But no, this was of a different sort. Danthres was asking about Sorlin with a constancy that bordered on obsession.

Well, no, that wasn't entirely fair. When she needed to focus on the case, she did, but for the long walk through the thoroughfares of Cliff's End, she started pestering him with questions.

"Did the council just *decide* to disband? How low had the population fallen, anyhow?"

"I do not know the specifics," Fanthral said tightly. "Perhaps you should send a message to someone you knew from there who would be able to inform you of the details. My reasons for being there were purely to seek out—"

Danthres waved a hand back and forth. "Yes, yes, I know what you were there for, your ridiculous hunt for former elf lords."

Tartly, Fanthral said, "It is not 'ridiculous.' The Elf Queen was not the sole actor in her tyranny. She could not have wielded the power she did, nor commit the despicable acts she committed, without the support and assistance of the nobility."

"Really?" Danthres gave Fanthral the same malicious smile that she gave to people in the interview room when she was about to nail them to the proverbial wall. "Did you not say to Torin earlier today that you were forced to mistreat human prisoners by the Elf Queen and that to do otherwise would be to court punishment of your own?"

Fanthral shot Torin a glance, which Torin pointedly ignored in his attempt to walk faster. He had nothing to add, and the only reason he didn't say what Danthres was saying now was because she'd beaten him to it.

Looking back at Danthres as they passed into Unicorn Precinct, Fanthral said, "I did say that to *Lieutenant ban Wyvald*, yes."

Realizing that he wasn't going to be able to stay out of it, Torin said, "The conversation was in a public place among three people. I was unaware that its contents were meant to be private."

"So," Danthres asked, "why aren't *you* being hauled up before this tribunal or whatever it is?"

"That is not your concern." Fanthral started walking even faster, passing Torin by.

Danthres called after him. "It is if we're supposed to be hauling ourselves all over the city-state on this pointless quest to find the nonexistent person who killed your elf lord!"

Fanthral said nothing in response.

"Leave it alone, Danthres," Torin said, just as she was about to open her mouth to say something else.

"Why should I?"

Torin smiled. "Because constantly antagonizing him is a poor way of getting him to tell you more about Sorlin."

She shook her head in disgust. "He doesn't know any more than he's telling me. It's not something he gave a shit about—no 'proper' elf ever did give a shit about Sorlin. He only gave a shit because a couple of his stupid elf lords wound up there and died like they should have."

"Well, then, why not do as he suggested?"

She looked down at him curiously. "Do what?"

"Send a message to a friend from there to see if you can get a more complete story."

That resulted in a scowl that would have done Osric proud. "That would require me to actually have a friend to contact."

With that, Danthres also strode ahead. Torin was now three strides behind his partner, and five behind Fanthral. Plus neither of them was talking anymore, so Torin supposed that he had gotten what he wanted, more or less.

They reached the castle after another few minutes, and Fanthral actually led the way to the winding staircase. Torin had to admit to being impressed with the elf's recollection of the castle's sometimes confusing corridors. Prior to coming to Cliff's End and working for the Castle Guard, Torin had spent his life living in the wide-open spaces and modest houses of Myverin, outdoors (occasionally, if he was very fortunate, under a tent) both after leaving Myverin and when he joined the army to fight the elven wars, and in the occasional inn during his other travels. None of that had adequately prepared Torin for the labyrinthine halls of the castle that served as the seat of Cliff's End. By now, of course, he knew his way around easily, but in the first year, he often got lost on his way from the squadroom to the privy.

Fanthral was the first one to arrive at the bottom of the stairs, where the large wooden door with the gryphon door knocker was wide open.

Boneen was standing over lothSerra's body when they arrived, and he looked up at Fanthral. "You must be the elven emissary."

"I am Fanthral. I am here to—"

"I am not interested in why you are here. Suffice it to say that this case has implications that are far more important than whatever witch hunt you might be on."

Fanthral snarled. "It is *not* a witch hunt!"

Torin, however, was more interested in Boneen himself. His white hair, normally wild and flying in all directions, was trimmed to a simple monk's fringe, and his white beard now only went as far as his throat instead of his chest. He wore the same drab, ill-fitting clothes he always wore, of course.

"I wasn't aware, Boneen," he said with a grin, "that meetings with the brotherhood had a dress code."

Boneen just gave Torin one of his trademark annoyed looks. "Bravo, ban Wyvald, you noticed that I cut my hair. That puts you one up on your captain."

"Well, I *am* a detective."

"Bravo for your ability to detect, then."

Fanthral looked as if he was about to crawl out of his skin. "May we please get back to Elthor lothSerra?"

"Ah, yes." Boneen waddled over to a stool and sat down. "Whew. That's better. It has been a very long and difficult day, and this elven corpse has increased that difficulty by a great deal."

Danthres was leaning against one of the lab's walls. "What did you find, Boneen?"

"This is my first examination of a body that has overdosed on this 'Bliss' substance. Indeed, it is my first examination of Bliss in any form. There was no need, really, since I have absolutely no interest in the myriad substances that people choose to eat, drink, inhale, or ingest in the name of briefly feeling better."

Torin smiled. "Which is why you don't generally accompany us to the Chain."

Fanthral shot Torin a look. "The what?"

"The Old Ball and Chain," Torin said. "It's a tavern where we tend to congregate after work."

"I see. If I may ask, what does any of this have to do with lothSerra?"

Boneen regarded Fanthral with irritation. "I'm getting to that, if you'll just give me a moment. Now, where was I?"

Danthres said, "Eating, drinking, inhaling, and ingesting."

Boneen snapped his fingers. "Yes, of course. Now then, the first thing I did when confronted with this body—"

Holding up a hand, Fanthral said, "Wait, you examined the body first?"

"Yes. If I may continue—"

"Why did you not meet us in Haven's Way? You were to perform a peel-back—"

"Which I will perform in due course," Boneen snapped. "However, I have already cast a Teleport Spell today that brought me from Barlin to here. Inanimate Residue is a complex spell, and Teleport is a powerful one, with the power increasing with distance. To cast both in one day is simply beyond my means."

Torin decided not to point out that Boneen had teleported to many a crime scene, performed the peel-back, and then teleported away. Besides, that was generally within the boundaries of the demesne, whereas Barlin was a two-week journey, so it wasn't really the same thing.

"I fail to see how—" Fanthral started.

Danthres pushed herself off from the wall and stood between Boneen and Fanthral. "Ignore this idiot, Boneen."

"Excuse me—" Fanthral started again.

However, Danthres just interrupted again. "What did you find?"

"Bliss is not a natural narcotic. It was created with magic."

Fanthral squinted with apparent confusion. "Aren't most recreational drugs of this sort enhanced by magic?"

"You're not listening!" Boneen was so agitated he almost fell off his stool. Torin moved to hold his arm so he could steady himself. "Thank you, ban Wyvald. In any case, my point is that it hasn't been *enhanced* by magic, it's been *created* by magic. Bliss is the creation of a wizard. And that's a problem."

"Who cares who created it?" Fanthral asked. "What matters is who gave it to lothSerra!"

"That matters to *you*," Boneen said tersely, "but of far more import to myself, and to everyone who is taking this drug in Cliff's End is who made it in the first place."

"Why is that, Boneen?" Torin asked.

"If a member of the brotherhood created something like this— in fact, if *any* wizard wished to create this—they would need sanction from the brotherhood, and I know for a fact that they don't have it."

Snidely, Fanthral asked, "How can you be so sure?"

Boneen closed his eyes and sighed. "As I was forcibly reminded recently, the brotherhood manages everything via committee. The sanction I mentioned comes from one of those committees, and I'm a member of it. So I'd know if something like this was submitted to the brotherhood. I'm afraid that Bliss is unlicensed magic, and it must be stopped."

Danthres closed her eyes and started rubbing the bridge of her nose between her thumb and index finger. "Please, Boneen, tell me you didn't alert Gunderson to—"

"I sent him a mage-bird shortly after I sent the one to you lot."

"Dammit!" Danthres pounded on the nearest surface, which happened to be the table lothSerra was on. "Now the brotherhood will stick their noses—"

Holding up both hands, Boneen said, "No, they won't. I've already spoken to Gunderson, and he assures me that he will not be inserting himself into the investigation. His exact words were that he prefers that those who were trained for such things handle it." He smiled. "I can only assume he meant you two."

Torin sighed. "That's something, at least."

"You must discover the source of this drug," Boneen said forcefully.

"As it happens," Torin said, "we have a lead on that, which we had just received when you summoned us."

Danthres nodded. "So it's back to Goblin to find Kempog and see if he's really the distributor."

"What if he isn't?" Fanthral asked.

Torin grinned. "Oh, worry not. We'll find *something* we can detain Kempog for, and then he'll either talk, or send one of his cohorts to find out what we need to know."

Fanthral moved toward the exit. "Then let us be off. I wish to find lothSerra's murderer once and for all!"

Danthres shook her head. "Idiot. And now we have this lovely new wrinkle."

"Here it comes," Torin muttered.

"I *hate* magic!"

Torin shook his head as he followed her out the door and up the staircase. His partner was eminently predictable. Sometimes that was even part of her charm.

TEN

ON OCCASION, KEMPOG WISHED HIS FATHER WAS STILL ALIVE SO HE could see how completely wrong he was about his son.

Those occasions were usually when he was drunk, of course. When he sobered up, he remembered that the happiest day in his life was when that old bastard finally drank himself into a well-deserved grave. After that wonderful day, Kempog no longer had to suffer his abuse, both verbal and physical—though the latter had waned somewhat since Kempog grew to his full height, which was exactly the same as that of his father.

The former, however, continued unabated until the day the old man finally died: "Y'shouldn't be around those people." "Getcher self a real job." "That ain't honest work." "Your mother woulda cried herself t'sleep, she saw you makin' a mess'a your life." And so on.

Plus, of course, Kempog's favorite: "Whyn'tcha go into construction like a *sensible* person?"

That was the worst part of all, once Kempog got big enough to no longer be beaten, his father's insistence that Kempog be like *every other dwarf in Cliff's End* and go into construction.

Kempog *hated* construction. Hated building things, hated carrying heavy things, hated physical labor, and, most of all, hated the risk of suffering the same fate as his father.

When Kempog had come of age, his father had been the victim of an on-the-job accident: a large piece of lumber fell off a wheel-barrow and crushed his leg. A healer had been called, and he managed to keep the old man from losing his leg, but he walked with a limp and could no longer do the job. They let him do some administrative stuff, at which he proved so awful that they let him go, but he'd been there long enough to earn a pension.

After which, he sat around and put that entire pension into ale. Mother was long dead by then, and Kempog had been working on the streets of Goblin Precinct.

"Go into construction," his father had said over and over again. "S'always gonna be good work. New people're movin' t'Cliff's End all'a time. An' it ain't like we're gonna run outta room—just cut down more forest."

That last part was something he always added after the one time Kempog made the mistake of saying, "Of course they're gonna run out of room, Father—there's only so much space between the castle and the docks!"

"Gumfingers!" his father would cry, his favorite interjection. "There's plenty'a room t'the west—jus' cut down more'a Nimvale. Ain't like nobody cares about no trees, and 'sides which, we need the lumber for more buildings!" That was followed by an open-handed slap to the back of Kempog's head.

He stopped questioning his father after that.

Meanwhile, Kempog started working as a runner for the various criminals who dealt in illegal spells and smuggling and so on. Eventually he worked his way up to a position of relative importance.

And then his father died. The last thing the old man ever said to him was a drunken slur: "Y've wasted y'r life, Kempog. Wasted it." Then he passed out, and never woke up.

If only his father could see him now.

Well, truth be told, his father would likely just complain that he wasn't in the wonderful occupation of construction, that bastion of good living that was so good to them that it destroyed his father's ability to walk, and led to his drinking himself to an early grave.

But still, he wished the old man had lived long enough to see Kempog walk into the house wearing a shirt made of silk instead of burlap, linen pants from Saptor rather than Barlin, and with more gold than silver in his pouch.

And he had the wizard to thank.

He generally didn't even like wizards. They were annoying, arrogant shitbrains who thought they knew everything, but mostly knew nothing.

Kind of like his father.

But not *his* wizard. No, *his* wizard was different—special. Not like the others.

Kempog was eating lunch at the small table he kept near the kitchen in the small house he'd purchased on Old Port Way. The way the gold was pouring in from Bliss sales, he'd be able to get a place in Dragon soon enough—maybe even a nice mansion in Unicorn!

That would be something—him, the person his father deemed a failure, living in Unicorn with all the nobility.

If sales kept up the way they were going, that would be possible in a few more weeks.

Everybody loved Bliss. Between his street smarts and the wizard's skill, they were all going to be very, very wealthy.

And by "all," he meant himself and the wizard. Sure, some others would benefit, like Urgoth, for helping out. But the dragon's share of the profits was being split between him and the wizard— right down the middle. That was their arrangement. After all, Bliss wouldn't have been any kind of success without his ability to sell it.

But before he'd met the wizard, Kempog wasn't much of anybody. Less of a nobody than he would have been if he'd taken his father's advice to help idiots put up more buildings in Cliff's End, but still not somebody people *talked* about. Or when they did, they talked about that low-life, that thug, that guy. When the Cloaks came 'round looking for info, they'd grab Kempog and find some excuse to hold him so he'd give up something on someone else. They used him, same as everyone else. When a guild needed muscle, or someone to find something a little less than legal, they paid him; when the Cloaks needed info, they "paid" him by not throwing him in the hole.

Now, though, he was paying himself. No more working for others. He was working *with* the wizard, and together, they were drowning in gold coins.

Just as he finished off the stew his cook had made for him—he had a cook now, which he really thought might have been the best part of being wealthier—one of his enforcers poked his head into the room. Kempog hadn't wanted to have bodyguards, but after the third attempted break-in by someone sent to learn the formula for Bliss, he realized he had to take steps. Luckily, old Mags Barstow owed him several favors, and she had several muscular sons and grandsons.

Kempog had been unable to keep their names straight, so he stopped bothering, going instead with what few distinguishing features were to be had in a collection of half-a-dozen inbred behemoths. The one he saw now was Cheek Mole.

"Urgoth's here."

That prompted Kempog to roll his eyes. He'd told all six Barstow boys that Urgoth should *always* be let in, but the notion of exceptions never seemed to penetrate what passed for their brains, and they always checked. Kempog just thanked Xinf that the wizard stayed in the basement working all the time and didn't go out hardly at all.

"Let him in."

"'Kay." Cheek Mole opened the door all the way and said, "Kempog says it's okay."

Urgoth came in, not even giving Cheek Mole a second glance. Urgoth and Kempog had grown up together, both sons of construction workers living on Kite Path. Urgoth was short even by dwarven standards, and the other kids always made fun of him, and beat him up. Kempog, though, always liked him because he was funny, and he would defend him against the bullies.

Unlike Kempog, Urgoth wanted to follow in his father's footsteps, but he was too small and frail to do the work. Kempog helped him out, throwing some work at him that he couldn't do, for whatever reason. Eventually, they became—well, not partners, exactly, because Kempog was always the main guy, but at the very least a team. Urgoth was often his helper.

So naturally, when he got together with the wizard, the first person he enlisted to help him out was Urgoth.

Things had been going so very well that Kempog found the concerned expression on Urgoth's face worrisome. "What's wrong, Urgoth?" Suddenly, Kempog was overcome with panic. "The deal with Gavin fall through?"

Shaking his head, Urgoth said, "Nah, that's all right. Gavin said he'll have gathered the necessary coin tomorrow."

"Good." Kempog was relieved. Gavin was buying a huge supply of Bliss to put on a ship and distribute out onto the islands in the Garamin. The wizard needed that cash in order to get some of the supplies needed to refine the process so that folks wouldn't be overdosing so much. Plus, they had advanced Gavin and his crew a portion of their load, and Kempog damn well wanted to be paid for that, at least. "So, what's wrong?"

"I was chin-waggin' with Nulti, right, an' we got us a bit of a problem."

Kempog nodded. Nulti was one of the guards they had on the payroll. Not the smartest guard ever, but he heard things that Kempog sometimes found useful.

"They got six more'a them ODs on Bliss."

Holding up a hand, Kempog said, "Yeah, yeah, I know, look, the wizard an' me, we're workin' on it, okay? That's why we need Gavin's coin. Once we figure it all out, nobody'll OD on Bliss." Of course, it was all the wizard, not Kempog, but he liked to create the illusion that he collaborated on that end of it as well.

And the deaths *were* a problem. Dead customers weren't repeat customers.

"Yeah, but people, they're talkin', right?"

"Let them talk." Kempog rose from his stool and started pacing the dining room. "Look, it's tragic, but people die in Goblin all'a time. Nobody's gonna give a shit about some people who die happy."

"It's ain't just that," Urgoth said urgently. "We got us a bigger issue, right. Elko? He's dead."

Kempog frowned. "Elko's that guy on Orphan's Way?"

Urgoth nodded. "See, I found out that he wasn't buyin' for his woman like he said he was. He was buyin' for Brindy."

"You told me you cut Brindy off."

"*I* did; Elko, he didn't. So I had to cut Elko off, right, and Brindy, he didn't like that so much, and Brindy went an' killed Elko."

Kempog was all set to dismiss Urgoth's concerns right up until he said the word *killed*. "You sure?"

"It's all *anyone's* talking about down Orphan's. An' they called the Swords in."

"So?" Kempog shrugged. "S'what we pay Nulti for."

Urgoth shook his head. "Swords called in the Cloaks."

That got a wince out of Kempog. the Swords were no problem. Most of them were underpaid, underappreciated, and overly greedy. But the Cloaks were another story.

Then a thought occurred. "Which Cloaks got it?"

"The older one."

"Iaian." Kempog sighed with relief. "He's bribeable."

"Not for murder, he ain't." Urgoth shook his head. "Look, we got us folks who're killin' each other. That ain't good. And somethin' else."

"Look, just slip a few gold to Iaian, make sure we stay out of it. Everything'll be fine."

"I toldja, there's more. Nulti heard that there's an elf followin' the half-elf bitch and her red-bearded partner around, and that they're lookin' at one of our ODs."

Kempog frowned. "An elf? Why does some elf give a shit about—?

"Dunno, but it ain't good. They took the corpse outta the body shop, and down to the M.E."

"So?"

Urgoth stared at Kempog as if he was insane. "If they look into it and find out about—"

"They're not gonna find anythin', all right? Besides, we ain't doin' nothin' illegal."

That didn't seem to placate Urgoth. "I think we oughtta think about movin' somewhere safer. Everybody knows you bought this place, an' if the Cloaks come lookin'—"

Walking over to his childhood friend, Kempog put his hands on Urgoth's tiny shoulders. "It'll be fine, Urgoth. You're worryin' way too much. All we're doin' is makin' people happy. Cloaks can't do *nothin'* to us. Now c'mon, let's go an' count today's haul."

Urgoth nodded, but Kempog could tell he wasn't happy. Usually, counting money put Urgoth into a good mood. Kempog was sure it would do the trick this time, too, especially since yesterday's take was just sitting there waiting for him and Urgoth to take care of it.

He grinned as they went into the counting room.

"Why're you smilin' s'much?" Urgoth asked snappishly.

"'Cause I got me a house with a counting room, so I can count all my gold." He sighed. "If only my father coulda lived to see this."

ELEVEN

W<small>HEN</small> H<small>AWK</small> <small>ARRIVED, ALONG WITH</small> D<small>RU AND</small> G<small>ROVIS, AT THE</small> A<small>XE</small>
Lane branch of the Cliff's End Bank, he was surprised to see Than
Martel there waiting for them.

When he was at Frannik's Lane earlier, Martel was tense; now,
he was in full-blown panic. He'd loosened his necktie, and Hawk
could see rivulets of sweat running down his long face.

As confused as Hawk was to see the bank manager here, that
was as nothing compared to Grovis's shock. Hawk had assumed
that each bank had its own manager.

And indeed, Grovis put his hands on his hips as they arrived at
the entrance to the bank. "Than? What are *you* doing here? You're
supposed to be at Frannik's Lane."

Dabbing sweat from his high forehead, Martel said, "I'm also
manager of this bank."

"I don't understand," Grovis said, "what happened to Yellin?"

"We had to let him go." Martel hesitated. "And Catlan and Hilig
as well. I'm now manager of all four banks."

"Erm, well, congratulations, I suppose, but dash it, Than—
Yellin, Catlan, and Hilig were good people! They—"

"I'm sorry, Amilar, but I really do not have time to bring you up
to date on personnel changes at the bank. If you *really* care that
much, please ask your father."

Grovis looked down and shook his head, muttering, "You seem
to speak to him more than I, lately."

While Hawk was enjoying the banter as much as anyone, they had a case to solve. "'Scuse me, Mr. Martel, but could you please be tellin' us what happened?"

"I don't know, I wasn't actually on-site. I thought you lot would be here sooner, to be honest."

Dru answered that. "We needed to make sure that nobody reported any coins covered in red."

"Stopped by Unicorn and Dragon, and they ain't heard a thing," Hawk added. "You'd think we woulda been hearin' *something*, seein' as that's your security, and all."

Martel winced. "Ah, yes, well, I'm afraid there's a bit of an issue, there."

"I should think," Dru said. "You didn't even *mention* that you had a security system in place. We only know about it thanks to 'Amilar' here."

"You see," Martel said, after wiping some more sweat off his forehead, "there's a very good reason why I did not mention the security system we have in place."

"And that's bein' what, exactly?" Hawk asked.

"It *isn't* in place, and hasn't been for over a month." Martel sighed. "For Ghandurha's sake, you *really* should talk to Mr. Grovis about this."

"Daddy isn't here," Grovis said tartly. "You are. And since you're the manager of this bank—indeed, of all four of them, apparently—then it behooves us to inquire of *you* as to why the security system that would have foiled these malefactors is no longer present!"

Hawk looked over at Grovis, impressed. The young lieutenant didn't usually get *this* pissed off, and it was kind of fun to watch.

"The bank—" Martel sighed. "Oh, for Ghandurha's sake, I really think—"

Dru stepped forward. "We can do this here or back at the castle, Mr. Martel."

"Very well." Martel held his hands together with fingers interlaced again. "You see, the bank has had some—some difficulties of late."

"Daddy never mentioned anything to me."

"I can't speak to that, Amilar, but it's true." He sighed. "Some of the bank's investments did not work out as planned. Some real estate loans on Oak Way were defaulted upon after the dragon attack at midsummer, some shipping concerns fell through, and so on. The wedding between your cousin and the Cynnis girl being called off, and the subsequent scandal with Sir Malik, was a terrible blow as well."

Grovis frowned. "I don't understand."

"Part of the terms of the marriage was that the Cynnis family would invest in the bank. Obviously, with the family having moved to Iaron under a cloud of scandal, that was no longer possible."

"Oh dear." Grovis frowned.

"I'm sorry," Dru said, "but what does that have to do with the security?"

Again, Martel sighed, which he'd done so much that Hawk was now pretty sure he could enumerate everything the bank manager had eaten that day. "The security requires a monthly fee to be paid to the Brotherhood of Wizards for its use. The fee is considerable, but one that the bank could afford easily *before* the recent troubles. Now, however, in order to maintain customer satisfaction—"

Dru chuckled. "You mean in order to be able to actually *fulfill* a withdrawal request?"

Shaking his head, Hawk said, "See, this is why I ain't trustin' no bank with my money."

Martel was just looking sick now. "It was a *temporary* situation until Mr. Grovis was able to find more investors. Indeed, Lady Meerka informed Mr. Grovis that she would match the stipend that comes with being a member of the court, as long as he used it to reinvest in the bank so—"

Dru held up a hand. "Okay, enough, we get it. No security, so these guys just waltzed in and took the money. We'll need to talk to whoever was here."

Hawk looked around and saw Jared, one of the guards assigned to Dragon Precinct. "Jared, c'mere a minute."

"Yes, sir, Lieutenant," Jared said as he approached, "what can I do for you?"

"Find a kid from the youth squad, and get 'em to head to the castle to be bringin' Boneen here."

Dru looked down at Hawk. "You crazy? Boneen's only just back, he ain't gonna—"

Hawk regarded his partner right back. "You even listenin'? Lady Meerka's gonna put her hard-earned gold coins into this here bank, and now it got robbed twice? We'll be needin' a peel-back, and damn fast."

With a sigh, Dru said, "Yeah, you're right. Fine, let's do that."

Jared nodded. "Right away, sir."

"All right, it's prob'ly gonna be as useless as it was the last time, but let's talk to some witnesses," Dru said, "and see what we got until Boneen gets his bony ass down here."

The sun was setting by the time Boneen deigned to arrive. In that time, Hawk had interviewed nine people, all of whom had stories that varied even more than the ones he heard at Frannik's.

There was only one consistency in the testimony: everyone commented on how *calm* the thieves were. Hawk was surprised to hear that, and even more so, when he, Dru, and Grovis compared notes after interviewing all thirty people who were present in the bank at the time of the robbery.

As Boneen waddled down Axe Lane to the entrance, Hawk smiled. "Good of you to be showin' up, Boneen."

"It was, I assure you, *not* my first choice. In fact, I almost turned the young man who was sent to summon me into a newt simply to teach him a lesson for rudeness." Boneen scowled. "However my incantation was interrupted by Sir Rommett, who insisted that I proceed immediately to Axe Lane to perform Inanimate Residue on a bank, the precise request made by the young man who came within a hairsbreadth of living his remaining years as a lizard." He held out his hands, which were smudged with herbs. "So here I am. Please have your thugs remove all persons from the bank."

Martel stepped forward. "I'm afraid that won't be possible, as someone *must* be present when—"

Hawk was looking forward to watching Boneen tear the bank manager apart, but Grovis stepped in, ruining his fun. "Than, I'm sorry, but the magickal examiner *cannot* cast his spell if there is anyone in the bank. You must evacuate it, and I mean *now*."

"Bank policy is that—"

Grovis then did something Hawk had never seen him do: he got in someone's face. "Bank *policy*? My good man, bank *policy* is not to be *robbed twice in one day*! Now then, Boneen—a mage on loan from the Brotherhood of Wizards—is here at the specific request of *Lady Meerka*. Are you telling me, Than, that you intend to deny him the ability to perform the very duty he was sent here to perform by *Lady Meerka*? Well? *Are* you?"

The sweat, Hawk noted, was now pouring down Martel's face, and he decided that this was even more fun than Boneen's scathing wit would have been.

Martel swallowed twice, then muttered, "Yes of course," and went into the bank.

Hawk looked over at Jared. "Go be givin' him a hand gettin' everyone out."

Nodding so enthusiastically his blond hair flopped, Jared said, "Absolutely, sir."

"A fine guard, that one," Grovis said, nodding at Jared. "I like the cut of his jib."

"I'll cut your jib in a moment," Boneen muttered. "I truly do not have time for this nonsense. There's unlicensed magic going on, and my services are required to investigate that, not deal with imbeciles who steal money from banks."

Boneen continued muttering and moaning for the next thirty minutes. Hawk could hear him through the bank's front door.

Once the half-hour had passed, he exited the bank.

"Uh oh," Dru said.

"What's wrong?" Hawk asked.

"Boneen." Dru shook his head. "Usually, when he's done with the peel-back he's either pissed and cranky, or tired and cranky. But look at him now."

Hawk regarded the wizard more closely. "He looks—I dunno, concerned?"

"Yeah." Dru folded his arms over the gryphon symbol on his chest. "Can you think of any way that Boneen looking concerned is a *good* thing?"

"There were four thieves," Boneen said as he waddled up to the lieutenants, "and they were using glamours."

"Yes, we're *aware* of that, Boneen," Grovis said haughtily, although this was their first confirmation of the number of thieves. "As they did at Frannik's Lane. But surely you can see through them."

"Under normal circumstances, I could easily see through a glamour—particularly cheap store-bought ones as these were."

Hawk let out a Martel-like sigh. "So why ain't these circumstances normal?"

"Because these thieves also had magic coursing through their bloodstreams."

"How is *that* possible?" Grovis asked.

Boneen shook his head. "Based upon my examination of Elthor lothSerra, I can say with surety that all four of your thieves were high on Bliss when they robbed the bank."

Dru looked at Hawk. "Well, that explains that."

"Explains what?" Boneen asked testily.

Hawk said, "The witnesses was even more useless than usual, but there was one thing they *all* be sayin' in common. The thieves, they was *calm*."

"I'm sure it made for a most pleasant robbery," Boneen said witheringly.

Grovis's mouth was hanging open the way it did when he was confused, which was, Hawk thought cruelly, most of the time. "I'm sorry, Boneen, but I'm afraid there's something I don't understand."

"Don't sell yourself short, Grovis," Boneen said. "There are many things you don't understand. From which of that legion of items do you wish to inquire at present?"

Drawing himself up to what passed for his full height, Grovis said, "I see no reason to stand here and be insulted!"

"Then I'll leave." Boneen started to turn around.

"No, wait!" Grovis cried. "I simply wish to know why you can't see through the glamours!"

Hawk nodded. "That's true, you ain't been explainin' that."

"Of course I have," Boneen said testily. "As I said, they were high on Bliss."

"What's that got to do—" Dru started.

But Boneen interrupted, waving his hand back and forth. "Right, of course, I forgot, you three weren't there. When I examined lothSerra's body, I discovered that Bliss was created with magic. And quite powerful magic at that—enough so that it distorts the peel-back and makes it impossible to poke through the glamour. I'm afraid the thieves' identity will have to remain a mystery until *you* three can find them." Boneen then smiled. "Which means it may well stay a secret until the end of time."

Dru snorted. "Yeah, real funny, Boneen."

"Thank you," Boneen said with no sincerity whatsoever. "Now if you'll excuse me, I'm long overdue for a nap or three."

Boneen headed back toward Meerka Way.

Hawk stared after him. "He *is* tired, if he ain't teleportin' back."

"Yeah." Drew clapped his gloved hands. "Actually, we oughtta be followin' him to the castle. We need to report to the captain and figure out our next move."

"I'm tellin' you what our next move oughtta be," Hawk said. "We got us two banks that got hit and two banks left."

"Uh, okay," Dru said slowly. "Not sure what—"

"I'm thinkin'," Hawk interrupted, "that these folks'll be hittin' the other two tomorrow."

Grovis put his hand to his chin, in what Hawk could only assume was an attempt to look thoughtful. "They might not even wait that long."

Dru shook his head. "Nah, if these guys were capable of breaking into a locked bank, they woulda done it last night. They hit both banks when they were open."

Nodding, Grovis said, "Perhaps, but it would, I think, be wise to have guards from Dragon on both the Auburn Way and the Hranto's Way branches."

Martel was hovering on the periphery of their little impromptu gathering, and he raised a hand and spoke. "Excuse me, but I think we should have guards on all four."

"They're not gonna come back to where they've already hit," Dru said impatiently, "they already proved that when they hit this place."

"We're talking about Bliss addicts, Lieutenant." Martel suddenly remembered what class he was, and started speaking haughtily again. "I doubt that rational logic will apply to them."

Somehow, Hawk managed not to say what he wanted to say, which was, "As opposed to irrational logic?" Mostly he just didn't want to talk to the irritating bank manager any more than necessary.

Dru looked at Grovis. "You mind headin' to Dragon and talking to Sergeant Kel about settin' that up?"

Grovis nodded. "Of course."

Hawk looked over at Jared. "You stay on point here 'till your shift's endin', all right?"

"Not a problem, Lieutenant," Jared said eagerly.

Then Hawk looked back at Dru and Grovis. "I'm thinkin' tomorrow, you and me, Dru, we stake out them other two branches."

Shaking his head, Dru said, "Even guys hopped up on Bliss ain't gonna hit a bank that has a guard standing right outside it. And we can't exactly hide wearin' full armor and a big-ass Cloak."

Hawk shrugged "We just gotta ask the cap'n for a coupla glamours."

"Yeah?" Dru snorted. "What's the backup plan for after he laughs in our faces?"

"You kiddin'?" Hawk pointed in the general direction that Boneen had wandered. "This case was enough to get Boneen down here when he wasn't in no kinda mood to move, and you *know* how hard it is to be gettin' his tiny legs movin' when he don't wanna."

"Yeah, okay, we should be able to get glamours." Dru turned to Grovis. "What time do the banks open?"

"Sunup, generally—isn't that right, Than?"

Martel nodded. "Assuming Mr. Grovis doesn't decide to shut them down."

"He ain't," Hawk said, "'cause we ain't lettin' him. Since the M.E. couldn't find nothin', only way we're gonna catch these shitbrains is in the act."

Again, Dru clapped his hands. "All right, Grovis, you take care'a Dragon. We'll head back to HQ." He grinned. "Betcha a copper we catch up to Boneen before we cross back into Unicorn."

Hawk grinned right back. "He wanted that nap too much to move slow, and you walk too damn slow anyhow. I'll take that action."

TWELVE

EVER SINCE HE WAS A SMALL BOY GROWING UP IN TREEMARK, SAM Brindl wanted to be a bard.

His family owned the Goblin's Teeth Tavern in the heart of Treemark, and Mother and Father had groomed him to take over from the moment he was tall enough to see over the bar.

But try as his parents could, they were never able to get him to be enthusiastic about tending bar, or serving customers, or doing the books, or any of the chores associated with keeping the Goblin's Teeth going.

Oh, he *learned* those tasks, as he was always a dutiful son. But he never embraced them with the enthusiasm that Father and Mother had hoped he would.

Every spare moment, though, that was spent with Honig, the bard who performed at the tavern most nights.

Honig was a tall, thin man with a thick beard and a mellifluous voice. He played a lute, and for a long time, Sam thought he was the best lute player in all Flingaria. Later in life, Sam learned better. While Honig was talented, and he always kept his lute more or less in tune, he was far from the finest. Over the years, Sam had heard dozens of lute players who made Honig look like a barely talented amateur—but when Sam was a boy? Nobody was better than Honig.

Every moment of spare time that Sam had, he spent with Honig, trying to learn what he knew. Honig showed him how to pronounce words clearly so that they could be understood, how to use the cadence of particular syllables to his advantage, how to use dramatic pauses and rhymes to good effect, how to listen for when the lute went out of tune, and so on.

And then, one horrible day, Honig left. He gave no notice, no warning, merely left a piece of parchment behind with the words, "Gone to Cliff's End. My best to young Sam."

Mother and Father were furious, especially since they hadn't had a replacement for that night's entertainment. They wound up hiring a terrible juggler, who didn't understand that free drinks were not part of his payment, and his bar tab exceeded his night's pay by a factor of ten—and then he refused to pay it, though Mother and Father didn't give him his pay, either.

However, Sam wasn't in the least bit surprised at the bard's departure, though he probably took it better because Honig actually acknowledged him in his brief goodbye missive. Honig had always talked about Cliff's End as being the best place to be if you were a bard. They had the most taverns, the most inns, and the most people coming through. "Here in Treemark, young Sam," Honig had always said, "you get lots of regulars, which means you have to keep coming up with new material. But in Cliff's End? The same tavern could have entirely different people from one week to the next. You can tell the same story, sing the same song, over and over again."

Sam had pointed out that part of Honig's appeal was that he always had new songs to sing and new stories to tell, but the bard's response had been, "Yes, but after a while, young Sam, you really start to run out of material."

That, Sam had never understood. There were so many great heroes, so many wars going on, so many battles being fought. Every day there was a new story from someone who came home from some war or other, or a traveling bard with some new tale.

Just as Sam envied Honig his life, Honig envied the traveling bards theirs. When Sam had asked him why he didn't become one, that bright smile would peek forth from behind that thick beard, and Honig would say, "I could never sleep out of doors, young Sam. I would fear a troll would eat me in the night. Better to stay under a roof."

After Honig's departure, Sam begged and pleaded with his parents to allow him to take over as the tavern's bard. They were reluctant, for his assistance was desperately needed around the tavern itself. Mother and Father were not getting any younger, after all, and their attempts to have additional children had all failed. In fact, one of the saddest songs Honig had ever sung was a haunting dirge he wrote in memory of Sam's stillborn little brother.

As a compromise, they let him perform once a week, while carrying out his other duties as waiter, bartender, and cook's helper as needed the rest of the time.

To everyone's surprise, he was quite popular. Sam was more surprised than anyone because, while he always dreamt of being a bard, he was never entirely sure he was any good at it. Yes, Honig had made encouraging noises, but Sam was his employer's only child, and Sam could never be entirely sure that Honig wasn't simply trying to stay in good with the people who put gold coins in his pocket. ("The tips are useful, young Sam, but the steady pay is what keeps a bard from starving.")

But while Sam couldn't hold the crowds the way that Honig could, they did applaud when he finished telling a story. It helped that he knew many of Honig's most popular tales, and Sam had even come up with a tune to sing one of Honig's spoken stories to, though he sang it unaccompanied, of course, since he didn't have an instrument of his own.

Mother and Father didn't pay him a salary, but he was allowed to keep his tips, and eventually he collected enough coppers (and even the occasional silver) to finally buy his own lute, so his songs could have music, and he could even sometimes strum to go with his spoken stories.

He kept abreast of current events as much as possible, telling tales and singing songs of some of the great heroes of Flingaria: from the noble Gan Brightblade to the mysterious Pirate Queen to the mighty King Marcus. When the infamous killer Bronnik was captured by agents of Lord Newcastle and Lady Belle, Sam had actually been commissioned by the Lord and Lady to compose a song celebrating the foul killer's capture and execution.

It was right after Bronnik's capture, however, that the fever spread through Treemark, and Mother succumbed to it.

Father was despondent after that. He barely spoke following Mother's memorial service, and the tavern went to seed fairly quickly. Drinks weren't restocked, waiters weren't paid, entertainers weren't hired. Sam tried his best to keep things running, but while he, Mother, and Father did well as a trio, all helping each other out, it was not a job one person could do alone.

Then one night, Father went to sleep and didn't wake up. The healer Sam called said he could find no cause for his death, but postulated that he simply died of a broken heart.

Sam hadn't realized you could die of such things.

He sold the tavern after he buried Father, and used the money to go to Cliff's End.

There, he knew, he could thrive. He just needed to find Honig.

Sam traveled in a caravan of coaches that was en route from Treemark to Cliff's End. Most of the passengers were people getting ready for sea voyages, or visiting people there. Only a few, like Sam, were intending to live there.

One was actually returning from a trip to visit family in Treemark, and he said that he had heard of Honig as the bard who sometimes played at the Ogre's Breath. Prior to that, he had played in the Dog and Duck. "The OB," as the man referred to it, was located in a region called "Goblin Precinct." Sam had no idea where that would be, exactly, but he was soon able to determine that the city-state of Cliff's End was divided into four sections named after various creatures, and that Goblin was where the less well-off of the city-state resided.

Sam was fine with that—after all, the poor needed somewhere to drink and be entertained, too—so when he arrived at the terminal clearing just outside the city-state's borders where all caravans ended (or started) their journeys, he immediately inquired about how to obtain a horse that would take him to Goblin Precinct.

He quickly learned that that would not be possible. The thoroughfares were too crowded to allow horses. If Sam had known he was going to have to walk through the entirety of the city-state, he wouldn't have brought quite so much of his stuff.

A gnome offered to store his luggage for a mere two silvers, and he and his friend took it all away, providing Sam with an address where he could pick it up later. It was only the next day that he discovered that the address didn't actually exist anywhere in Cliff's End. The member of the Castle Guard to whom he reported this crime informed him that his possessions were likely being sold on Jorbin's Way.

But Sam's disappointments were only beginning. He arrived, after a lengthy and tiring walk, at the Ogre's Breath only to discover that Honig no longer worked there. A particularly surly bartender informed him that the bard had been arrested following a brawl. That had rather surprised Sam, as the bard had always been a peaceful sort, but he supposed that Honig might have been trying to break it up and was arrested along with the true malefactors.

After being told in no uncertain terms that no, the Ogre's Breath was *not* in the market for a new bard, Sam walked some more, this time to Goblin Precinct headquarters. A sergeant whose name he never got directed him to a female guard who appeared to be half-elven and half-human. She was also the single ugliest woman Sam had ever seen in his life, and that was after living for almost twenty years with his mother.

"Honig?" she said. "Oh, you mean that untalented drunken shitbrain that they hired to pretend to sing at the OB? Every witness we spoke to after that brawl last week said he started it." She snorted, a very unpleasant sound, and added, "Not that it takes much to start a fight at the OB. Anyhow, I sent him to the hole, and a buncha people filed a complaint, so I had to kick it over to the detectives, since I'm apparently not worthy to fill out boring paperwork." She sounded more than a little bitter. "If you want to know what happened to that drunken shitbrain, talk to Lieutenant Iaian in the castle."

That led to another lengthy walk, this time all the way to the seat of the city-state—a castle located right near the clearing that had served as the terminal. Sam was allowed to see this Iaian person, who wore similar leather armor to that of the guards he'd met at Goblin Precinct, but with a gryphon emblem on the chest instead of a goblin, and Iaian also wore a brown cloak.

"Yeah, I took care'a that. It was weird, 'cause I been in the Guard for coming up on ten years now, an' they've been fightin' in the OB for all that, but this is the first time anyone actually put in a *complaint*. It was weird. So I had to take it off Goblin's hands—after listening to that bitch guard. What the hell's her name, Tresyllione?" Iaian shrugged. "But anyhow, it wound up not matterin', 'cause Honig hung himself in the hole."

That nearly caused Sam to faint right there in the castle. Iaian looked annoyed, and he got his partner—an elderly gentleman named Linder—to assist him.

Honig's personal effects had been confiscated by the Castle Guard and auctioned off to line Lord Albin and Lady Meerka's treasury, so Sam had nothing to remember his mentor by.

On Linder's recommendation, Sam went to the Dog and Duck—which, he recalled, was the last place Honig worked before he went to the Ogre's Breath—and met with Olaf, the owner, a bald man with a thick black mustache.

"Hiring a bard, I am not doing," he said. "Sorry, sorry, but after Honig I swear off bard forever. They are worth less than they are trouble, yes?"

Sam didn't understand, as he could testify to Honig's talents, but Olaf just shook his bald head.

"Fine, he was, at first, but Honig, he start to drink, and then downhill was all that it went to."

That, at least, explained why that guard woman—Tresyllione?—called him a "drunken shitbrain" not once, but twice.

Sam's attempts to explain his own teetotaling lifestyle fell on deaf ears. "Honig, he say the exact same words to me when he arrive. I not be fooled a second time," Olaf said while wagging a finger in Sam's face.

Disheartened, Sam moved on to several other taverns, before finally being hired by the Stone Kobold. Sam performed three times a week right under the object that gave the tavern its name.

On the night of his third performance, a man came running into the Kobold crying, "The war's over! The Elf Queen is no more!"

As the night progressed, more people came in saying things like the Elf Queen was dead, or the Elf Queen had gone into hiding, or the Elf Queen had abdicated her throne—but it all boiled down to the fact that the war was over.

The next ten years were simply *awful* for Sam. Peace spread throughout Flingaria. The Elf Queen's defeat ended the elves' imperialism, King Marcus and Queen Marta's forces were so devastated by the fighting against the elves that any thoughts of war needed to be put aside, and the dwarves just wanted to live in peace, which they finally could with the Elf Queen's defeat.

Which was all well and good for the people of Flingaria, but it played merry hell with a bard's ability to make a living. People got tired of hearing the same old tales and the same old songs.

It wasn't so bad at first, of course. There were lots of songs to be sung about the final battles, and the triumphant return home of all the soldiers and heroes who won the war. Olthar lothSirhans— the nephew of the Elf Queen, whose betrayal of his aunt was the key to victory—alone was good for half a dozen songs.

Initially, the very thing that attracted Honig to Cliff's End, to wit the heavy turnover of clientele in the taverns, worked in Sam's favor. But as time went on, the Kobold modulated into a neighborhood tavern with a cadre of regulars. And they quickly grew weary of hearing the old standbys over and over again.

Sam kept trying to find new places to work. He occasionally would be hired by some rich family or other to perform at an event, and of course every midsummer he'd sing songs on Meerka Way for tips.

But steady work proved impossible to come by. The Kobold reduced his frequency to twice a week, then only once, eventually letting him go all together. He managed to survive—barely—on the occasional wealthy patron, but those gigs were few and far between. When Olaf remodeled the Dog and Duck, he advertised for a singer, and Sam auditioned for the gig, but it went to a younger bard. "His songs, they are new, yes? I like songs that were invented since the time my nephew, he was born."

Then the Pirate Queen seemingly disappeared—no one had

heard of any new exploit from her or her crew in years. King Marcus grew old and became more a ruler than a general. The dragon who came every midsummer burned down a house on Oak Way; rumor had it that the Brotherhood of Wizards had gotten rid of the ancient creature after that, which may well have meant a cancelling of the largest festival in Cliff's End, with a concomitant loss of income for Sam.

Worst of all, Gan Brightblade and Olthar lothSirhans died. They didn't even die heroically, they were just murdered by a person seeking pitiful revenge for a nonexistent slight. Try as he could, Sam could not find a way to compose a compelling melody around that.

Not that his melodies were anything to cheer about. His best material was about Bronnik, but no one outside of Treemark cared about him. As time went on, he became more despondent. Worse, his fingers started to shake, and his ability to play the lute deteriorated to the point where he had to go back to performing unaccompanied.

He had no idea if he could possibly go on living.

Sam had gone from renting a small house in Dragon to a small flat in a building in Dragon to a smaller flat in a building in Goblin to a corner of a room in a tiny house in Goblin. Down the street from that tiny house lived a dwarf named Urgoth, who sometimes threw some coppers at Sam in exchange for his song about Bronnik. (Urgoth had no idea who Bronnik was, beyond what the song itself told him, but he really liked the melody.)

One day, Urgoth saw how miserable Sam was, and he offered him something that would make him feel better. It was just a pill, but Sam figured he had nothing to lose. It was worth a copper, and Urgoth gave that to him in lieu of payment for singing the song about Bronnik.

And he felt *fantastic*!

The last time he felt this good, he was back in Treemark in the Goblin's Teeth, and he'd finished his day's work of cleaning the bar and all the tables and then Mother and Father would smile at him and say it was okay to go sit with Honig and the bard would show him how to finger another note and they'd practice the evening set together and then he'd watch Honig perform while waiting tables and everybody clapped and Sam would dream of some day being up there on the stage and singing and telling stories and getting applause and it was simply glorious!

And then the pill wore off and he remembered that Mother and Father and Honig were all dead, that the Goblin's Teeth was now an eatery called the Suckling Pig, and that Sam was an aging, arthritic bard with no prospects in a world that was fast running out of things to sing about.

He went to find Urgoth that night to give him all the coppers he had in his money pouch—which, sadly, was only thirteen—in exchange for thirteen pills.

"All right," Urgoth said, "that should hold you for a couple of weeks."

In that, Urgoth was wrong. Sam took all thirteen pills at once.

He was happier than he believed it was possible to be, right up until he died.

THIRTEEN

HAWK SCOWLED AS HE SAT IN A CAFÉ LOCATED ON AUBURN WAY across from the branch of the Cliff's End Bank. To anyone walking past, he was a haughty-looking elf. Hawk had never had much time for elves, and doubted he could convincingly sound like one.

At that, he was lucky. He could've looked like a gnome.

Captain Osric had agreed to let them use glamours in order to keep the two remaining branches of the bank under surveillance. "But they have to be pre-set glamours. We don't have the budget for an open glamour."

Sergeant Jonas had sent one of the guards to purchase one, and Micah returned with two glamours, as requested. "'Fraid they only had these two left at Minar's," Micah said. "One's an elf, one's a gnome."

Dru looked incredulously at the guard. "You're tellin' me Minar's only had *two* glamours in the whole place?"

Micah shifted his weight from boot to boot. "Er, well, not exactly, sir, but—well, I assume you wanted *male* glamours, yeah?"

"Good assumption, yeah," Dru muttered.

Osric was scowling, like usual. "You have what you need. Take them, go home, get a good night's sleep, and stake out the banks tomorrow. I assume there are guards on the bank tonight?"

That question was directed at Grovis, who was seated at his desk. "Yes, Sergeant Kel said he would arrange it."

Osric looked over at Iaian. "What about your murder?"

The older detective leaned back in his chair. "We're lookin' for a guy named Brindy. We got his description out to all four precincts—though I doubt he'll be anywhere other than Goblin or Mermaid." Iaian then explained about Brindy and Elko and their arrangement regarding the acquisition of Bliss.

Shaking his head, Osric muttered, "An elf lord dead of a Bliss OD, bank robberies by people high on Bliss, and people getting murdered over Bliss. If we find out who's manufacturing this, I may personally run him through."

With that, Osric wandered back to his office, probably to sharpen his dagger some more.

Micah stared at Dru and Hawk. "So who gets what?"

Hawk blurted, "I'm takin' the elf!" at the same time that Dru said, "Gimme the elf."

They stared at each other.

Then Dru took out a copper. "Flip you for it?"

Hawk shrugged. "Sure."

Dru pocketed the copper before flipping it. "Hang on, we caught up to Boneen, so you owe me a copper."

Hawk sighed. He was never gonna save up for his boat if he kept losing bets to Dru like this. "Fine." He removed a copper from his own pouch and handed it to his partner.

"Call it," Dru said as he tossed it in the air.

"Heads."

It landed on the floor of the squadroom with a *ping*, the profile of Lady Meerka looking up at them.

Hawk grinned and held his hand out to Micah. "The elf, please."

Now, after going home to take care of his father and get a good night's sleep—during which he dreamt about the boat—he sat in a café trying to look haughty so people would believe he was an elf.

For most of the morning, nothing happened. People walked into the bank, people walked out of the bank. Hawk was quickly growing incredibly bored. He started thinking some more about the boat, wondering what he should name her. Currently, it was called the *Starlight*, but Hawk thought that was a dumb name for a boat. Maybe he could call it *Sword and Sorcery*? No, that was even dumber. *Alone at Last*? Tempting, but a little too obvious.

Perhaps he could just call it *Retirement*.

Then he saw it: four people who all looked exactly alike. They were walking casually together up Auburn Way, heading straight for the bank. Hawk stared intently at them: they all had *exactly* the same face. Each was a nondescript, pale-skinned human.

None of them appeared armed, but neither did Hawk. His glamour was hiding the very large sword at his side, so it only stood to reason that the thieves' glamour worked similarly. They entered the bank together.

Dropping some coins on the table, Hawk strode away from the café as fast as he could, following the foursome inside.

As soon as he entered, one of the thieves pointed a longsword at him. Two of the others had swords out, as well—one a broadsword, the other also with a longsword—with the fourth holding a dagger at the throat of someone in a suit.

"Nobody move!" Dagger cried. "I'm gonna kill this guy if anybody *moves*!"

Hawk's hand was moving toward his currently invisible sword, then changed his mind. The bank employee's life was at stake. "I'm sorry," he said, "I didn't know that—"

"*Shut up!*" Broadsword yelled. "Get your ass over there with the rest of the people!"

Hawk took in the scene. There were six people off to the side. Two wore suits similar to that of Dagger's hostage, so they were probably the other employees. This was a small bank compared to the other two—the space was less than half that of the Frannik's Lane location—and after Martel's comments yesterday, it didn't surprise Hawk that they only had three people working there.

The other four were a dwarf woman and a pair of gnomes, the latter two appearing to be a couple, since the two men were huddled together.

Hawk slowly walked over to join them.

"All right," Dagger said, guiding his hostage toward the back room, "give us *all your gold!*"

"O-o-o-okay, just p-please don't c-cut m-my thr—"

"Just *move!*"

Broadsword walked over to Dagger while holding a large burlap sack.

Longsword One stood near the seven hostages and looked over at Longsword Two. "Check the door, make sure nobody else comes wanderin' in."

"Why do I gotta do that?" Longsword Two asked testily.

"'Cause I *asked* ya to, shitbrain! Now move it!"

Longsword Two spit on the floor and then went to stand by the door.

Hawk didn't think he was going out on much of a limb by hypothesizing that these guys weren't hopped up on Bliss the way they were at the Axe Way robbery yesterday.

While standing at the door, Longsword Two said, "Dunno why you're bossin' me around anyhow. Gavin's the boss."

Longsword One didn't look at his friend as he replied, keeping his eye on the hostages. "An' Gavin's in the back room, so out here, *I'm* the boss. You got a problem with that?"

"Yeah, actually, I do! You and me, we joined up with Gavin at the same time. An' it was your stupid idea to take the stuff they advanced us, 'stead'a givin' it to Cap'n Bridgers like we were s'posed to. S'why do I gotta—"

"Just shut *up*, already!" Longsword One finally turned to look at his comrade. "We can fight this out *after* the robbery, okay?"

"Fine." Longsword Two was pouting now.

Now Hawk had more information. Dagger was probably this Gavin person, and they were working with Captain Bridgers. If Hawk remembered correctly, he was the shipmaster of the *Amarilla*. Even if he wasn't able to capture these guys now, he had a name and someone they could question.

Broadsword came out hauling the burlap sack over his shoulder. It jingled as he walked. Dagger—or, rather, Gavin—came out behind him. Gavin's blade was still at the employee's throat, which now had a trickle of blood mingling with the poor man's sweat.

Gavin then threw his hostage at the others. His two fellow employees caught him awkwardly, all three of them stumbling and nearly falling to the floor, managing to steady themselves on a nearby desk.

"C'mon, let's get outta here." Gavin moved quickly toward the door, the others following suit.

Now that there wasn't a life directly in danger, Hawk made his move, gripping the glamour in such a way that it would deactivate.

"Castle Guard—don't be movin' a muscle!" To punctuate his point, he unsheathed his sword, which came out with a metallic scratch that usually got people's attention.

"Shit!" Longsword Two cried. "See? See?"

"Shut up!" Gavin said. "It's four on one, Cloak."

"Not for long," Hawk said. "When I took off my glamour, that alerted every guard in Dragon that I'm in trouble." That was a stretch of the truth—the only one who'd be alerted was Dru, but he'd come running quickly, dragging along as many of Dragon's guards as he could. Hawk just had to hold these guys off for a little bit.

Gavin stepped forward. "Seriously? You think you can take us down?"

Hawk also started moving forward, bringing him and Gavin closer to each other. "What I 'think' is that you four just robbed your third bank in two days, and that that ain't entirely legal. What I 'think' is that you fellas are in some serious shit because you're messin' with the place that holds a lotta money belongin' to a lotta rich people who get all cranky when folks mess with their coin. What I 'think' is that your stupid ass shouldn't be lettin' me get so close."

And with that, Hawk ran Gavin through with his longsword.

Hawk had been in the Castle Guard for almost a decade, including tours in Unicorn and Mermaid before being promoted to lieutenant. In all that time, he had never actually used his sword. Indeed, he could count the number of times he went so far as to unsheathe it on the fingers of one hand.

He hadn't really expected to use it now. But Gavin had kept moving closer to Hawk, and Hawk had kept moving closer to Gavin, and all Hawk could see was Gavin's dagger blade drawing blood from a poor innocent bastard whose only crime was to come to work in the morning, and Hawk just found that he had to run the shitbrain through.

Gavin fell to the floor, bleeding rather profusely from a chest wound. Hawk couldn't keep his grip on the sword hilt, the blade seemingly stuck in Gavin's body as he collapsed. Blood continued to gush from either side of the blade as Gavin stared blankly at the ceiling, gurgling up blood.

The other three just stood in shock for a bit. So did Hawk, suddenly realizing just what it was he had done and not entirely sure what should be done next. After all, robbing banks wasn't generally a capital offense. On the other hand, threatening the life of a lieutenant in the Castle Guard most definitely was, and Hawk doubted the magistrate would accept the argument that Hawk was in disguise, and therefore they didn't know they were threatening a guard.

Then Broadsword cried out, "He killed Gavin!" showing that he had a facility for the obvious.

Longsword One then said the words Hawk had really been hoping he wouldn't say: "Get him!"

What followed was a mass of arms and legs and blades and pain as Hawk found himself knocked to the floor and screaming with pain as fists collided with his face and against his body. The latter didn't hurt so much thanks to his armor.

But all three were on top of him. He raised his arms to protect his face, but fists and booted feet collided with him constantly.

"Hold him down!"

Four hands pinned his shoulders to the floor. Hawk struggled, pushing against the restraint and failing to move.

Then he felt something cold inside his chest. Only after that did he notice that Broadsword had impaled him in the chest.

Oddly, while he ached from all the blows he'd just taken, being stabbed in the chest with a large sword *didn't* hurt. He really thought it should have.

"*Hawk!*"

That was Dru's voice, although Hawk couldn't see him to verify it. He did see Broadsword—who, he supposed, would need a new nickname—get clobbered by someone wearing leather armor with a dragon emblem on the chest. And no one was pinning down his shoulders anymore.

And then there was Dru, kneeling by his side. "Oh shit, Hawk, what the hell happened?"

"Boss—" Hawk then coughed, the salty taste of blood accompanying the cough.

"Don't try to talk." He looked up. "Get a healer over here! *Move!*"

Hawk grabbed Dru's chest, clearing his throat, trying to talk past the blood. "Gavin's—boss—killed him. Workin' with—Cap'n Bridgers—*Amarilla*."

"Stop tryin'a talk, dammit, you need to save your strength."

"Dunno why—why I killed—Gavin."

"It's okay, partner, really. You had your reasons. Don't worry about it. We'll get a healer down here and you'll be *fine*, you hear me?"

Hawk could no longer see Dru, only knew he was still there from the sound of his voice and his own hand on his partner's chest.

"Talk to me!" Dru cried.

"I—" Just that one syllable prompted another coughing fit, and now Hawk's mouth filled with blood, so much so that he feared he would drown in it. A roaring started in his ears that made Dru's voice recede into the background.

"C'mon, Hawk, stay with me. Where's that damned healer?"

"Tell—tell—Dad—I—"

But Hawk couldn't make the words come out. He wanted Dru to tell his father that he loved him, and he forgave him for all the years of living off Hawk and pretending to be sick.

Then he couldn't hear anything at all, besides that awful roaring in his ears. The pain was gone, too, from the beating.

His last thought was regret that he never did figure out what to name the damn boat.

FOURTEEN

THE RAID ON KEMPOG'S PLACE OF BUSINESS WAS HELD FIRST THING IN the morning. The role that Bliss played in lothSerra's death, as well as that of Iaian's murder on Orphan's Way, meant that Kempog was a person of interest in at least two cases.

Torin wasn't too keen on the notion of referring to lothSerra's death as a case, but they did have paperwork on it that would be filed with Ep, the imp who kept all their case files in interdimensional storage. Still, suicides and accidental deaths—and lothSerra was one or the other, Torin was sure of it—did not fall within the Castle Guard's purview. It only mattered because of the elf's status.

However, Iaian's main witness mentioned a dwarf named Urgoth, and two of Goblin's guards—Allard and Brenn—confirmed that Kempog didn't take a shit without Urgoth offering him a wipe. Kempog was walking around with a lot more coin, Urgoth was connected to the sale of Bliss, and the sale of Bliss was what led to Elko's death. So even if it didn't matter to his and Danthres's not-really-a-case, it did matter to Iaian.

So rather than report to the castle, Torin and Danthres—the latter having spent the night with the former, as they were wont to do on occasion—together went to Goblin, where they met Iaian and Grovis, along with a contingent of guards with goblin emblems. With Dru and Hawk off on their stakeout of the only Cliff's End Bank branches not to be robbed yesterday, there was no formal roll call and morning rundown, which Torin knew had to be driving Sergeant Jonas mad.

"Why so many for this raid, again?" Danthres asked.

Grovis said, "If this Kempog fellow is turning into a bigger fish in the criminal pond, he might have some protection."

"He isn't a criminal," Torin said impatiently, "he's a flunky who's gotten above himself. And while he's probably connected to Elko and possibly connected to IothSerra—"

"And also connected to the robberies of Daddy's bank!" Grovis put in. "Boneen *did* say that the thieves were high on Bliss, after all."

"Half of Goblin's high on Bliss. That doesn't prove that Kempog did anything," Torin said stubbornly.

"We still need to question him," Grovis said.

Danthres sighed. "Much as it pains me to agree with Grovis, he's right. In fact, he's right twice over. If he's suddenly throwing gold around, he's painting a target on his face. If he's smart, he's hired people to protect him."

Iaian shook his head. "I dunno, Danthres, I've met Kempog. That's a *big* 'if.' That shitbrain doesn't have the smarts that Wiate gave a gnat."

"Which begs the question," Torin said thoughtfully, as this hadn't occurred to him until just now, "how did he find himself a wizard to create unlicensed magic?"

"Only one way to find out." Danthres let loose with her most unpleasant smile.

That fell fairly quickly when Fanthral entered Goblin Precinct's front door.

"What's *he* doing here?"

Torin grinned. "Only one way to find out."

"Very funny."

The elf approached the four detectives. "I'm pleased that I'm not late. I only learned of this raid from your sergeant this morning, and I got down here as fast as I could."

Danthres regarded Torin. "Remind me to kill Jonas."

"Don't forget to kill Jonas."

Rolling her eyes, Danthres said, "Thank you *ever* so much. Who fed you wit this morning?"

"Punch him in the stomach, maybe he'll throw it back up." Iaian smirked as he headed toward the exit. "C'mon, let's get this over with."

Torin followed Iaian, with Danthres and Fanthral trailing after them. Grovis and the five guards from Goblin that Sergeant Markon had assigned followed along as well.

One of those guards, Kellan, walked alongside Torin. "I'm glad I got to come along."

Behind him, Danthres spoke before Torin could. "Why? I can guarantee that very little of interest will happen except that maybe we'll get to beat up whichever thugs Kempog has hired to protect his precious pill."

"I just like having a chance to help you all out. When Captain Osric transferred me to Goblin, he said this was the next step to joining you guys."

Again Danthres interrupted before Torin could speak. "Osric said he'll make *you* a detective?"

"When there's an opening, yes."

Danthres glanced at Grovis. "Well, they will make just about *anyone* a detective, so I suppose you'll do. Better you than Manfred, in any event." With that, Danthres used her long legs to stride ahead.

Kellan asked Torin, "I thought she and Manfred were . . ." He trailed off.

Torin shrugged. "Your guess is as good as mine, and I spent last night in her bed." Manfred, a guard currently assigned to Unicorn, had expressed an attraction for Danthres, which was rare indeed. They had spent some off-duty time together, but Danthres had refused to speak of it.

As nine people in the distinctive leather armor of the Castle Guard, four of whom were wearing the earth-colored cloaks that indicated the rank of lieutenant, strode down Old Port Way, accompanied by a fierce looking elf in armor of his own, people quickly moved out of their path. Torin saw fear in the eyes of many, defiance in the eyes of others. Whatever the initial response to their approach, it always modulated to relief when they passed by.

Nobody wanted to be the target of whatever it was that contrived to get nine guards together.

"Why is this called Old Port Way anyhow?" Grovis asked. "It isn't anywhere near the port."

"It used to be," Iaian said in the long-suffering tone he often used with his partner, "back before they built the new port where the docks are now. But the end of this road leads to a natural port that they used to use before the city-state got all built up and they needed something bigger. This used to be the path that led to it."

"Huh. I had no idea."

Iaian sighed. "Yeah, can't imagine why you'd have any idea that Old Port Way was the way to the old port."

"I see I'm not the only one who swallowed wit," Torin said to Iaian with a smirk.

"Yeah. This is the place," Iaian added as they came to a clapboard house with a small porch.

There were two very large young men sitting on that porch, and they got up as soon as they saw the guards approaching. Iaian and Grovis had taken point, since it was more about their case than the one Torin and Danthres were working.

One of them, the one with the mole on his cheek, said, "You can't come in here."

"Actually, we really can," Iaian said.

Grovis added, "We are the Cliff's End Castle Guard, here on the business of the Lord and Lady, and we may go as we please."

"I dunno 'bout that," said the other one, who had a scar on his forehead, "but Kempog says we can't let nobody inside, an' if anyone tried to get in that he don't want in, we was to kill 'em."

The one with the mole added, "An' Kempog definitely don't want no Swords nohow."

"All right," Danthres muttered to Torin and the guards, "let's get ready to take these two out before—"

Kellan stepped forward. "Hang on, I know these two."

Danthres stared at him as if he were mad. "From where, the All Brawn No Brains Club?"

"No, from the old neighborhood. Their ma's old Mags Barstow.

She used to live next door." Kellan stepped forward past Iaian and Grovis. "Walt, is that you?"

The one with the scar squinted. "Kelly? Shit, what *you* doin' here?"

Danthres looked at Torin and mouthed the word *Kelly*? Torin just shrugged.

"I'm in the Castle Guard now. Look, we need to talk to Kempog."

Walt shook his head very fast. "No. Nuh-uh. No way, Kelly, can't do it. Kempog's real partic'lar 'bout who he sees."

"Yeah, well, the Guard's particular about who they talk to, also. And we're kinda allowed to talk to whoever we want."

"Look, Kelly, I'm sorry, but it just ain't gonna happen."

"I'll tell you what *is* gonna happen." Kellan leaned in and stage-whispered to Walt. The other one, with the mole, he leaned over to hear what Kellan was saying, too. "There's nine of us here. Any of us get hurt, the whole rest of Goblin's gonna come crashing down on this place. But I don't think we *are* gonna get hurt. Lemme guess, Kempog hired you and Borak here, and I'm bettin' that he also got Lam and Zeek and Efram and the twins."

Borak shook his head. "Not Efram. He done went an' died on account'a he fell in the Garamin and drowned-like."

Kellan put a look of sympathy on his face. "Oh, I'm real sorry, Borak. Efram was a good kid."

"But yeah," Walt said, "we all here."

"So that's, what, six of you? There's nine of us. And I know Mags grows 'em big, but I still don't think that you boys'll come out on top of that one. And even if you do, eventually, you'll just wind up in the hole. What's Mags gonna say when that happens, huh?"

Borak looked at Walt. Walt looked at Borak. Torin could see them trying desperately to form a thought process and mostly failing.

"Ma wouldn't get mad at us," Borak finally said.

Kellan gave Borak a dubious expression. "C'mon, Borak, I went to the same spring and summer dinners you did, and what did old Mags always say?"

Speaking in frighteningly perfect unison, Borak and Walt both said, "'If you get put in the hole, don't come cryin' to me, 'cause I ain't gonna be your ma no more.'"

Pointing at them, Kellan said, "Exactly! Now if you don't let us in to talk to Kempog, we're gonna have to put *all six* of you in the hole. And then, poor old Mags ain't gonna have *any* kids left. Do you wanna do that to her?"

The two behemoths shuffled back and forth on their huge feet. Torin watched the tableau with intense curiosity. If they could get in without any violence or having to arrest anyone, it would be a significant coup for them. Arrests would just mean more paperwork. Plus, if the whole family was like these two, they might not *fit* in the average cell in the hole.

No, better to do things peacefully. He just hoped these two were up for it.

After a moment, the Barstow boys stepped aside. "All right, Kelly, we'll do it for Ma."

Borak stayed on the porch while Walt opened the door.

"Thanks, boys," Kellan said. "Old Mags'd be proud of you."

Torin said to Brenn, "You four stay out here. Keep an ear out in case this goes poorly."

Danthres meanwhile walked up to Kellan. "Not bad. That was almost intelligent."

Kellan actually rolled his eyes, though he waited until Danthres couldn't see him. Torin gave him an encouraging smile. He would indeed make a good detective, if this was any indication. Not that Torin was expecting an opening any time soon. Iaian was still a couple of years from retirement, Grovis seemed to be permanently ensconced no matter how incompetent he was, and Dru and Hawk were still fairly young.

They entered a sitting room, where two more incredibly large young men were seated, playing dice on a wooden table. Amazingly, these two looked almost exactly like Borak and Walt, except one was missing an eye and wearing an eyepatch to cover it, and the other was missing the fingers from his left hand (but not the thumb).

Eyepatch and Fingers both stood up upon their entrance. "Hey, Walt, whadja let 'em in for?"

"It's all right," Walt said. "It's Kelly."

They both stared at Kellan for a second, then all three eyes widened. "Shit, Kelly, what're *you* doin' in guard armor?" Fingers asked.

"Right now? Needin' to talk to Kempog. We need to know about two people he knows, Brindy and Elko."

"I dunno, I don't think Kempog'll—"

Walt interrupted Eyepatch. "It's okay, Lam, I got this. C'mon, Kelly, Kempog's in the dining room."

Torin walked past the two Barstow boys, who were as big as their brothers or cousins or whomever outside.

"You have to wonder," Danthres muttered, "if this Mags person drowns her offspring at birth if they aren't big enough."

Torin snorted.

Walt led them through another room, and another, before reaching the dining room, which adjoined the kitchen. The house was built with each room following the next, with no hallways, a style Torin had never liked.

Inside the dining area, two dwarves were sharing a stew. Iaian stepped forward and said, "Kempog, you're coming with us to the castle. We need to talk to you about some things."

One dwarf—Torin could only assume it was Kempog—stood up and ignored Iaian, instead glowering at Walt. "For Xinf's sake, what the hell am I paying you for? You keep asking me if I want Urgoth to come inside, but you let *these* people in?"

"They woulda taken us to the hole! And then Ma wouldn't love us no more!"

Kempog put his head in his hands.

Danthres smiled. "It is *so* difficult to find good help."

Fanthral then decided to step forward. "You will answer for your crimes, dwarf!"

"Will someone tell me what's going on?" Kempog asked. "You got no business here."

"Actually, we do," Iaian said. "We need to talk to you about a guy named Elk—"

He was interrupted by Fanthral, who said, "You poisoned an elf lord! Who is your employer?"

Torin winced. Fanthral was not helping.

Kempog shoved a tiny finger into Fanthral's chest. "I ain't workin' for *nobody*! Not ever again!"

"Yeah, with Bliss in your pocket, I don't doubt it," Iaian said. "Why else would you have the love children of a troll and a dockworker out there?"

Torin, though, was focused on a door to his right. The structure didn't have a second floor, and the dining room ran the width of the house, so that door had to lead to a basement.

He walked toward it, prompting the other dwarf, Urgoth, to speak for the first time. "Oi! You can't go down there!"

"I am afraid, good sir dwarf, that we may go where we wish when investigating crimes for the Lord and Lady, and we have come across a large number of them relating to Bliss of late."

Urgoth shook his tiny head. "You ain't gettin' me, Lieutenant. I ain't sayin' you ain't *allowed* down 'ere, I'm sayin' you *can't* go down 'ere. Wizard's got it all warded up and such-like."

"Dammit, Urgoth!" Kempog screamed.

Danthres walked over to Torin. "Warded, huh? I *hate* magic."

Torin scratched his thick red beard. "It does pose a bit of a problem. This confirms that Kempog is working with a wizard, and we'll need to question him. For that matter, so will Boneen."

"*That* ought to be amusing," Danthres said with a snort.

"The question is how to get a warded door open. I'm loath to bring Boneen down here for that."

"He's had all night to rest," Danthres said.

Meanwhile, Kellan was leading a complaining Kempog toward the front of the house, and Grovis was doing the same with Urgoth.

While Torin was trying to figure out how much he'd need to tip the youth squad to get Boneen here as fast as possible, Danthres said, "Someone's coming up the stairs."

Torin's less sensitive hearing didn't hear it until the footfalls were almost at the door, which was then thrown open.

Behind it was someone dressed in an approximation of the baggy robes worn by wizards, with fingertips smudged with the residue of spell components, and vaguely smelling like soil as they all did.

This one, however, did not have a beard, which was traditional—mainly because a far more prevalent convention was being thwarted with this particular wizard.

She had curly brown hair that—as was typical for a wizard—flew out in all directions. Her round face was centered with a button nose, and she had prominent cheekbones. Her figure was muted by her loose clothing, but she was definitely a woman.

"What is all this noise, Kempog? I told you, if you want me to perfect Bliss in time for Gavin's shipment, I need quiet."

Torin looked at Danthres. Danthres looked at Torin. They both looked at the woman.

However, it was Grovis who asked, "Are you a wizard?"

"Of course I am, you idiot. And you would appear to be detectives in the Castle Guard. You have no business here, as we have done nothing that violates the Lord and Lady's laws."

"But—" Grovis was goggling now. "But, you're—you're a *woman*!"

"No wonder they made you a detective." She turned to Torin and Danthres. "I presume you two are the brains of the outfit?"

"Lieutenant Torin ban Wyvald, and this is my partner Lieutenant Danthres Tresyllione. And I'm afraid you're going to have to come with us."

"My name is Morenn, and I told you that neither I nor Kempog have broken any laws."

"Maybe," Danthres said. "Yes, Bliss is legal, but actions relating to it aren't—including murder."

Torin moved toward her. "I'm afraid I'm going to have to insist that you come with me."

Morenn folded her arms over her chest. "And if I refuse?"

"Then we return with our magickal examiner. He's a member of the *Brotherhood* of Wizards."

At that, Morenn's face fell. "Very well, I will accompany you. But I see no reason to waste time on foot."

She gestured, and they all disappeared.

FIFTEEN

"Captain!"

Osric sighed heavily. He'd been enjoying the peace and quiet of the morning, at least in part because he knew it couldn't possibly last. It never did.

From the time he was old enough to hold a sword, Osric had been a fighter. At his parents' urging, he enlisted in the army so that the fighter could become a soldier, and therefore put his instincts and his desires to a more noble purpose.

But the life of a fighter, or of a soldier, or of a guard captain, was almost never a quiet one. So when an opportunity like this morning came, with all his detectives off on cases first thing, Osric always made sure to appreciate the silence.

Micah's voice echoing across the squadroom broke it, of course. Something always did, and this one had actually lasted longer than most.

With a heavy sigh, he got up from his chair and went out into the still-empty squadroom. Micah was standing at the western door that led to the rest of the castle. Of Jonas there was no sign, which Osric took as his sergeant recognizing that the captain wished to be left alone unless it was absolutely necessary and making himself accordingly scarce.

Whatever snide comment Osric was going to make, however, died on his lips as soon as he saw the stricken look on Micah's face. A former sailor who had been one of the few survivors on the *Erstwhile* when it was trapped in the Garamin during the last hurricane, it took a great deal to faze this particular guard.

"What is it, Micah?" Osric prompted when no further words were forthcoming.

"It's—I'm sorry, sir, but it's Lieutenant Hawk."

Even as he asked, "What about him?" Osric knew, just *knew*, what the answer would be. He'd sent far too many people to their deaths over the years not to know the signs.

"He's—he's dead, sir. It happened at the bank. That's all I know."

"Mitre's bones," Osric whispered. It was an oath he hadn't uttered since Lieutenant Linder was killed trying to break up a brawl on the docks. Osric's relationship with Mitre was complicated, as he'd had a hard time maintaining his belief during his life as a soldier, but whenever a comrade died, he always commended that person's soul to Mitre's care with that oath, taught to him by his father.

Just as he was about to cross the squadroom, a flash of light burst forth from somewhere inside it. Osric held up a hand to shield his eye.

When the light faded, Osric saw four detectives, five guards, two dwarves, General Fanthral, and a curly-haired human woman in brown robes. Since Boneen was nowhere in sight—and was down in his lair in any case, Osric assumed one of the dwarves was the wizard. But no, they were both restrained, one by Kellan, the other by Grovis, and you couldn't cast Teleport unless your hands were free.

"Now then," the woman said, "if you'll excuse me."

Then she made the same gesture that Osric had seen mages make dozens of times.

A second later, magickal bands of energy appeared as suddenly as the light from the Teleport Spell had, engulfed the woman's hands and feet, pulling them apart as far as possible, and suspended her half a leg above the floor.

Tresyllione was now doubled over, wretching onto the floor, as she always did when she was teleported. One of the guards was doing likewise.

"What in Mitre's name is going on here?" Osric asked, his second invocation of Mitre in the past four years.

"Release me this *instant!*" the curly haired woman screamed.

Osric looked at ban Wyvald. "Is that a *female* mage?"

"It would seem so, yes, Captain."

The woman snarled. "Are all of the Castle Guard this stunned by the obvious?"

"No," ban Wyvald said, "but we do comment when we encounter something we've never seen before."

Osric rubbed his temples with his fingertips. He'd gone from blessed quiet to insanity in less than a minute.

Just as he was about to speak, Boneen waddled in. "What has happened here, why has my defense spell been—?" He looked at the woman. "Who are you?"

"My name is Morenn, and I demand that you release me from this trap!"

Boneen stared at her for a moment. "That 'trap' is activated automatically when someone other than me uses magic within these walls. Did you purchase a spell?"

"Hardly," she said contemptuously.

"She *is* a wizard, Boneen," ban Wyvald said. "In fact, she is the wizard you have been seeking, as she's responsible for Bliss. It would seem that she created it, and Kempog here," he pointed at one of the dwarves, "is selling it for her."

Kempog spoke up, trying and failing to leap out of Kellan's grip. "I ain't doin' nothin' *for* her—we're workin' together! We're *partners*!"

"Shut *up*, Kempog!" Morenn cried.

"This is very bad," Boneen muttered.

"You don't know the half of it." Osric straightened up, hoping to regain control of the situation. "All right, listen to me, all of you. I was just informed that Lieutenant Hawk was killed."

That resulted in a cacophony of utterances, screams, shocked cries, and whatnot.

"*Quiet!*" Osric yelled at a volume he hadn't had to use since the war.

Everyone shut up then, though he did notice a knowing look on ban Wyvald's face. He'd been on the receiving end of that yell any number of times in the old days.

"I don't know the specifics as yet, but I do know that we must deal with that, and right away. We're going to Auburn Way to find out what happened—including you, Boneen."

"Hardly." Boneen put his hands on his hips. "This woman must be questioned immediately."

Fanthral stepped forward. "Since the death of this Lieutenant Hawk, while tragic, has nothing to do with my mission, I will remain and question this woman and her dwarves."

"I ain't 'her' dwarf!"

Osric ignored Kempog. He thought quickly, not about to let Fanthral loose in the squadroom without adult supervision. Besides, the king and queen themselves were pressuring Albin to cooperate with Fanthral, and Osric couldn't afford to completely ignore that. "Fine. Tresyllione, you'll stay with him and question these three."

"What?" Tresyllione said raggedly from her desk chair, onto which she had collapsed after throwing up.

"Captain—" Boneen started, but Osric cut him off, speaking in a very low, even tone.

"Understand something Boneen, and understand it well. Some-one killed one of my lieutenants, and there is *nothing* happening anywhere in this city-state, or anywhere in all of Flingaria, that is more important to me than finding the shitbrains who did it and putting them in the hole. That means that you will come with us to Auburn Way and cast a peel-back on the bank *right now*, so we can learn everything we can about them and bring them before the magistrate. Do I make myself clear?"

With a sigh, Boneen said, "Oh, very well. But I will meet you at the bank—I'll teleport there after I have informed Gunderson."

"Boneen—" Osric started, but this time the M.E. did the inter-rupting.

"When this great a violation of the brotherhood's bylaws occurs, I *must* report to the local representative *immediately*. Failure to do so will, I assure you, have far greater consequences to me than anything *you* could do."

"Don't be so sure of that," Osric muttered. One of the reasons why the Castle Guard was able to function as a law enforcement agency at all was because everyone in Cliff's End knew that you did *not* harm anyone wearing that leather armor, and woe be to anyone foolish enough to do so. The two sailors who were responsible for Linder's death were brought before the magistrate, condemned to be hanged, and executed within a day of the event, the fastest such had ever happened in the demesne's history. If Osric had his way, Hawk's murderer would feel the hangman's noose even sooner.

However, he did understand that Boneen had people to report to as well—people who could easily turn Osric into a farm animal.

Regarding Boneen harshly, Osric said, "You will be at the bank within the hour, Boneen, or the brotherhood will need to send us a magickal examiner who hasn't had his throat slit."

"Worry not, Captain, I have no desire for this conversation to go on any longer than necessary." He gazed disapprovingly at Morenn. "I hope you appreciate the mess you've started, young woman. I was hoping not to have to go through this again."

"There have been other female mages?" ban Wyvald asked.

"More than the brotherhood would have you believe," Morenn said with a fine sneer of her own.

Boneen shook his head. "Last time, I suggested that we simply make the woman into a man—such spells *do* exist, after all—but the notion was soundly and, if you ask me, unfairly rejected."

Osric looked over at the guard holding Kempog. "Kellan, you and Micah stay here and help Tresyllione in whatever way she needs. Everyone else, with me."

As he exited the squadroom, trailing his subordinates behind him, Osric found himself once again remembering *why* he reveled in those rare instances of peace and quiet . . .

SIXTEEN

Dʀᴜ ʜᴀᴅ ɴᴏ ɪᴅᴇᴀ ʜᴏᴡ ʟᴏɴɢ ʜᴇ'ᴅ ʙᴇᴇɴ sɪᴛᴛɪɴɢ ᴏɴ ᴛʜᴇ ғʟᴏᴏʀ ᴏғ the Auburn Way branch of the Cliff's End Bank, cradling Hawk's head in his lap.

He was going to have to tell his wife. Worse, he was going to have to tell Hawk's father. That old man was actually going to have to stop pretending he couldn't support himself. True, he'd get his son's pension, but Hawk hadn't even been with the Guard for a full ten years. You needed twenty to vest any kind of pension, twenty-five for a full one. The twenty-year pension was sufficiently meager that Iaian was hanging on long past his desired retirement date so he could get the twenty-five. A nine-year pension was basically nothing.

But that was the old man's problem, and not Dru's. Besides, all that coin that Hawk had been saving up for that stupid boat was probably under a mattress somewhere in his flat. The elderly bastard could live on that.

Not that Dru cared. What he cared about was that his partner was dead.

After everything they'd been through, to have it end like this. So many times they'd had each others' backs: their first case together, stopping those grifters who'd been working the docks, when Dru had almost drowned, and Hawk jumped into the water and saved him. That shitbrain who was kidnapping rich girls and killing them after the ransom got paid, who nearly slit Hawk's throat before Dru got the drop on him. The drunken soldier who tore apart the Stone Kobold, and almost did the same to Dru and Hawk both. The elf and dwarf who got into that fight during midsummer. And, of course, the Corvin case. That one nearly got both of them killed.

And now he was dead.

A hand touched his shoulder, and Dru looked up to see Torin's kind face looking down at him. "I'm sorry, Dru, but you need to get up."

"I can't leave him, Torin. I just—"

"You must. Boneen just arrived to cast the peel-back."

Dru nodded, understanding. The peel-back wouldn't work if there were any living beings in the range of the spell besides the spellcaster.

Of course that meant that Hawk didn't have to move at all.

Torin held out a gloved hand, and Dru clasped it, letting his fellow detective pull him to his feet. As he steadied himself, he saw the body on the ground, a Guard-issue longsword sticking out of its chest. When he first ran into the bank, the only thing Dru even noticed was his partner dying on the floor, so he didn't really take in the rest of the scene.

"That the thief?"

"One of them," Torin said. "According to the witnesses, there were four. That one was the ringleader, and was apparently named Gavin. Hawk killed him, and his friends killed Hawk."

Dru stared at Torin. "We gotta get these shitbrains. I knocked one of 'em down, but they all got away. We gotta get 'em, Torin!"

"We will—as soon as we get out of here and let Boneen do his work."

Nodding, Dru said, "Yeah. Yeah, right. Okay." He let Torin guide him out of the bank just as Boneen came in.

The next half an hour was the longest of Dru's life. Various guards kept walking up to him and expressing condolences and declaring that they'd "get the bastards" and so on. They were mostly a blur of platitudes and nonsense. Grovis's, in particular, seemed to go on for weeks.

Then Captain Osric walked up to him.

"Dru."

"Cap'n."

"I just want you to know, Dru—"

The lieutenant held up his hands. "Look, Cap'n, I appreciate what you wanna say, but I've been listenin' to everyone tell me they're sorry. I don't think I can stand anymore, and I don't want you tellin' me how much you want me to go home and not worry about nothin', and—"

"I'm not saying any such thing, Lieutenant."

That brought Dru up short. "You're not?"

Osric shook his head. "I'm not going to tell you what to do right now. I am going to tell you that, whatever you decide you have to do next, I'm behind you. And so is the rest of the Guard. You understand me?"

Relief spread over Dru. He had truly feared that the captain would send him home.

Torin walked up to them. "I just spoke with Allard and Brenn. They've been going door-to-door to see if anyone saw where the remaining three thieves went. They have a woman who assures them that the thieves went into a small hovel at the end of Yocane Way."

"Good," Osric said.

"It gets better." Torin smiled grimly. "One of Afrak's informants says that Gavin was in the midst of putting together a very large deal—*and* that he and his crew have been using a hovel at the end of Yocane Way for their base."

"So what the hell're we waiting for?"

"Me, for one thing," came Boneen's voice from the bank entrance. Turning, Dru saw the wizard walk slowly out. He seemed very tired—not the fatigue he usually affected in order to get people to feel sorry for him, or at least not ask him to do anything, but genuine exhaustion.

"What did the peel-back tell you, Boneen?" Osric asked.

"Four men wearing glamours entered the bank and took the half-dozen or so occupants hostage. Hawk entered, also wearing a glamour." He scowled at Osric. "A rather bad one, I might add. You really should give your people *good* glamours."

Osric ground his teeth. "Get on with it, please."

Boneen folded his tiny arms over his chest. "In any event, the dead one had a dagger to an employee's neck, so Hawk didn't act until everyone was out of immediate danger. Then he dropped the glamour and attempted to talk the thieves down. But the dead one kept moving closer, and finally Hawk ran him through." Boneen then opened his mouth and shut it again.

When Boneen's hesitation threatened to go on forever, Dru said, "Just get on with it, Boneen!"

"Yes, well, after that, the other three did rather pile on."

"Do you know which one killed Hawk?" Osric asked.

Boneen nodded. "One did run him through with his sword. I was able to penetrate the glamours this time—the Bliss in their system was all gone, for some reason—so I have descriptions of all of them. I'll transfer them to gems to distribute to the guards as soon as I can get to a scrying pool."

"Do that," Osric said.

"I will, and then I must speak to Tresyllione and that idiot elf." Boneen sighed. "The brotherhood is not pleased about this Morenn woman."

"She seems to be quite an accomplished mage." At Dru's confused expression, Torin added, "Bliss was created by a female wizard."

Dru blinked. "There are female wizards?"

"Apparently."

"Not according to the brotherhood." Boneen sighed, then spoke as if quoting something. "'Women do not have the requisite strength of will to perform the disciplines of magic.' Why do you think we call it the *Brotherhood* of Wizards?"

"And yet," Torin said, "there she is, creating drugs and teleporting a dozen people at once."

"Yes, well, it's an imperfect world," Boneen muttered. "I'll have Jonas send someone with the gems once they're done."

Then, after a few gestures, Boneen was gone in a flash of light.

While Dru blinked the spots out of his eyes, Torin said, "Captain, I see no reason to wait for Boneen's gems. We have a location, and with their ringleader dead, those three might not remain there for long."

Osric nodded. "Agreed. Let's go."

Dru watched as Osric and Torin gathered up Grovis and Iaian and the guards from Goblin who were hanging around waiting for someone to tell them what to do.

Within minutes, they were all walking in force down Yocane Way, passing the assorted ramshackle structures that the poorer folks of Cliff's End were forced to live in. Each guard had his sword unsheathed, which was not standard procedure. Osric had given no order to do so, nor had he told anyone not to do it—it was simply something everyone did as soon as they were en route.

All the people on the streets got out of their way. Dru recognized a couple of shitbrains from his days walking patrol in Goblin, the type of guys who'd eyefuck a guard just to show that they didn't give a shit about anything, and were tougher than the armored guys carrying swords.

But not today. Right now, those guys ran inside, praying to whichever god they believed in, and probably a few that they didn't, that they weren't going to be on the receiving end of their wrath.

Afrak was leading the way, and the short guard said, "This 'ere's the one."

Dru looked at Osric. "Cap'n?"

Osric pointed at the hovel's front door. "All yours, Lieutenant."

His sword firmly gripped in his gloved left hand, Dru thought about knocking on the flimsy wooden door, then rejected the notion.

Instead he kicked at it, and it flew completely open. Dru ran in, raising his sword, ready to take out whoever got in his way.

Nobody said anything. Nobody responded to his actions.

He ran into the hovel's only real room, a large area that had a bunch of throw cushions, a basin, and a wood-fire stove.

Lying on three of the cushions were three men, with big, goofy smiles on their faces.

One of them waved at Dru. "Hi there! Wow, there sure are a lotta ya."

For several seconds, Dru stood there, still holding his sword.

"You guys wanna take a seat?" another asked.

Only then did Dru register that some of the others had come in: Torin, Afrak, Grovis, Osric, and Iaian. Nobody else would fit.

Dru looked down at them. "Did you three rob the Cliff's End Bank?"

The third one bit his lip. "Yeah, sorry about that. We didn't mean to, but we didn't have no other way'a gettin' the money we needed for the deal with Kempog. See, we was gonna buy us a whoooooooooole lotta Bliss, and then take it out onto the *Amarilla* to sell out on the islands. It was a *great* plan! Gavin put the whoooooooooooooooole deal together!"

"Uhm," the first one said, "we prob'ly shouldn't be tellin' stuff like that t'the Swords. I mean, they don' like it when people rob banks."

"Or kill one of our own," Dru said tightly.

The second one smiled. "Oh, you mean the guy with the dreadlocks? He kinda killed Gavin, which was a total bring-down, y'know? So we hadda do somethin'."

"It wasn't really fair, though, was it?" the first one asked. "I mean, there was three of us an' only one'a him."

"Yeah, we should apologize to him when we see him next."

Dru just stood there in open-mouthed stupefaction.

Afrak put a hand on Dru's shoulder. "Been seein' this for a month now, Lieutenant. These shitbrains're Blissed out. Ain't gonna get nothin' useful out of 'em."

"Yeah." In fact, they got plenty out of them, as they'd just completely confessed.

But they were just so—so *relaxed* and happy. Dru had wanted desperate bank robbers, confused and angry after their job went bad, who'd put up a fight so Dru would have an excuse to beat the shit out of them.

He had no idea how to respond to this.

Luckily, Osric did. "Gather these three happy idiots up and bring them to the castle. They just confessed in front of plenty of witnesses. I can't imagine the magistrate will take long to condemn them."

Shuddering, Dru then said, "Yeah, Cap'n."

This wasn't how he wanted to avenge Hawk's death.

SEVENTEEN

WHEN JONAS BROUGHT DANTHRES THE HOT MUG OF TEA, SHE reached for it eagerly. "Thank you, Jonas. I *hate* magic."

"So you've mentioned," the sergeant said before dashing out of the squadroom, his green cloak billowing behind him.

She was standing outside the third interrogation room, leaning against the door for support as she sipped the herbal tea, hoping that it would cure the rumbling in her stomach.

"How much longer—" Fanthral started, but then Danthres just looked at him, and he slumped his shoulders. "Very well, we shall wait until you are ready." He shook his head. "But I must know why Elthor lothSerra was targeted."

Danthres was too queasy to argue that this was a fool's errand all over again. Besides, she was hoping he might relent and tell her more about Sorlin.

Then his ranting gave her a better idea. "Actually, Fanthral, I'm going to need a few more minutes for my stomach to settle. Why don't you go ahead and start questioning her?"

Fanthral straightened. "I would like that very much. Thank you, Lieutenant—I'm grateful, truly."

With a bit of a flourish, Danthres opened the door to the interview room to let him in—and then kept it open, standing just outside and to the left so that the occupants couldn't see her in the corridor, but she could still hear everything.

Morenn spoke as soon as Fanthral entered. "I hope you're the person in charge of getting me out of these restraints."

"I'm afraid that lies within the purview of the Brotherhood of Wizards."

"Of *course* it does. Well then, let me assure you that I have committed no crime and you have no business detaining me."

"I'm afraid *that* lies within the purview of the Castle Guard."

"So you're neither a wizard nor a guardsman. What *is* your function, exactly?"

"I serve the Elven Consortium."

Danthres heard Morenn snort. "Is *that* what the elves' latest pathetic attempt at a government is calling itself?"

Ignoring the dig, Fanthral said, "I have been tasked with retrieving members of the Elf Queen's court and bringing them home for war trials."

Morenn chuckled. "You've learned my secret—I'm actually Idiot lothMoron in disguise, cleverly hiding from my past crimes in service of the Elf Queen by posing as a female wizard, because that's a disguise *guaranteed* to give me a low profile."

Danthres smiled with admiration as she swallowed more tea. She liked Morenn's style.

"Do not toy with me, woman, or—"

"Or you'll imprison me in the castle in eldritch restraints?"

Fanthral said nothing in response to that, and Danthres had to force herself not to laugh out loud.

After several seconds, Morenn asked, "I've been alive for some thirty years, Mr. Elven Consortium, and in all that time, I've never even set foot in elf country. I've never even been as far west as the Nemerian Wastes. I can count the number of elves I've had dealings with on the fingers of my hands and I can assure you that none of that tiny number were of noble birth. I therefore can conclude wholeheartedly that I have no business whatsoever with you."

"So you deny that you were hired to give this Bliss of yours to Elthor lothSerra so that he would overdose on it and die before he could answer for his crimes?"

Another snort. "If someone had paid me to do that, I wouldn't need to rely so much on that stupid dwarf."

Gulping the last of her tea, Danthres made note of the fact that

Morenn and Kempog's relationship was not the most cordial. That would be useful.

"In any case," Morenn continued, "I've been working to fix the escalation problem with Bliss that leads to overdoses. I don't *want* people to die, I want people to be happy. That was the whole point. I don't know who Althor lothSeer even is, and—"

"It's Elthor lothSerra," Fanthral said tightly.

"I don't care if it was Olthar lothSirhans himself. The point is I don't know him, I can't help you, and I won't talk to you any longer."

"You will tell me what I wish to know, woman! Who targeted lothSerra?"

Morenn did not reply.

"Answer me!"

Still nothing.

Then Danthres heard the sliding-metal sound of a sword being removed from a scabbard, which was her cue to enter.

Morenn was hovering in the air, still bound by the magickal restraints, hovering near the small wooden table. Fanthral was standing before her, his sword out.

"Fanthral, that's *enough!*"

"I am handling this, Lieutenant." Fanthral did not look at Danthres, instead staring at Morenn with fury in his eyes.

"No, you're not. You're here as a courtesy extended by the Castle Guard, and you just used all that courtesy up. Get out."

Fanthral continued to not move.

Danthres sighed. "This woman is wanted for questioning by the brotherhood. Do you really wish to get on their bad side?"

That got Fanthral to lower his sword.

"C'mon." Danthres led him out the door and closed it.

As soon as the door shut, she smiled. "Thank you, Fanthral, that was *perfect.*"

The elf opened his mouth as if he was about to yell at Danthres, then shut it again and looked at her in confusion. "I'm sorry?"

"I'm grateful to you for softening her up like that. It'll make my part easier."

"I—"

"Ah, Tresyllione." Turning, Danthres saw that Boneen was entering the squadroom. He was looking even more wiped out than he had after coming back from his wizard meeting. "How fares our guest?"

"I'm about to talk to her. What happened with Hawk?"

Boneen quickly filled Danthres (and Fanthral) in on the events that took place on Auburn Way that morning.

"Damn," Danthres muttered. She'd always liked Hawk. He was only an okay detective, but he and Dru did their jobs well. They were certainly more palatable than the past-it Iaian and the never-had-it Grovis. He deserved better.

"Now that I'm done with that, I need to deal with that woman."

Danthres frowned. "What do you mean by 'deal with'?"

"The brotherhood has declared that all traces of Bliss must be eradicated, and that the woman in there—"

"Her name is Morenn," Danthres said.

Boneen nodded. "That Morenn must be delivered to them posthaste."

"And how exactly are you going to accomplish that?"

Frowning, Boneen said, "Delivering her is as simple as—"

Danthres waved a hand across her face. "No, no, not that part, I mean eradicating all traces of Bliss. I don't know *that* much about magic, but isn't that the sort of thing that the original spellcaster needs to do?"

The sour expression on Boneen's face answered Danthres's question for her.

She went on: "So you need her help."

"I suppose I do, yes." The reluctance in Boneen's voice was palpable.

Shaking her head, Danthres said, "That's just typical. You won't even let this woman into your precious cabal, yet you have to beg for her help before you condemn her."

"She came pre-condemned, Tresyllione. As I explained to your partner, it's called the Brotherhood of Wizards for a reason. Our official position is that women do not have the requisite strength of will to perform the disciplines of magic."

"What utter shit."

"Well, of *course* it's utter shit!" Boneen shook his head. "But there's precious little I can do about it."

Danthres put her hand to her forehead in disgust. "I knew the magickal community thought poorly of women, but I had no idea that you'd codified it."

"We're wizards, Tresyllione, we codify *everything*." Boneen sighed. "In any case, there's nothing for it. I must get her to eliminate Bliss, and then take her to Gunderson."

"Good luck with that." Danthres barked a laugh of derision. "She won't help you."

"She won't have a choice."

Fanthral finally said something. "The lieutenant is right. This woman is stubborn, and I doubt that even you could get her to cooperate."

"But I might be able to. Can you remove the restraints about ten seconds after I walk in?"

"Of course I can," Boneen said. "Why would I want to?"

"Because unlike you or Fanthral, I'm a practiced interrogator. I've spent the last decade going into that room and getting people to do things they don't wish to do. It's usually to confess to a crime, but this will be much the same thing."

Boneen regarded Danthres dubiously, then let out a long sigh. "Oh, very well, you may give it a try. But understand something, Tresyllione—while the brotherhood wants both the drug eliminated and Morenn in their clutches, they'll settle for the latter. Unlicensed magic is a sad reality that the brotherhood will live with if they have to. A woman mage, however, is something for which they have absolutely *no* tolerance."

Danthres nodded, as if understanding, though she in fact didn't comprehend it in the least. She approached the door. "Ten seconds after I shut the door, drop the restraints."

"Very well." Boneen started muttering something to himself, no doubt getting the spell ready so he could speak the final syllable at the appropriate moment.

Danthres re-entered the room, shutting the door behind her. Morenn still hung in the air near the table, the room's only lantern casting a large shadow that looked like a manta ray on the back wall.

"At last, someone in authority."

"I'm Lieutenant Danthres Tresyllione. Would you like to be free of your restraints?"

"A great deal, yes."

"Very well." Danthres snapped her fingers, just as her ten seconds expired.

The restraints faded to nothing, and Morenn fell toward the floor, but Danthres reached out to catch and steady her.

"Thank you." For the first time, Danthres heard something other than anger in the woman's voice. Her gratitude was genuine. "You're a woman."

Danthres smiled. "And you say the detectives are observant. But yes, I am a woman. Please, have a seat." Ignoring the uncomfortable stool on the other side of the table where suspects usually sat, Danthres instead indicated one of the two comfortable chairs that were there for the detectives. When she and Torin worked together in here, of course, they used both chairs, though rarely did they both sit at the same time. Constant movement did wonders for keeping suspects from feeling at ease.

But for this interview, Danthres wanted Morenn very much at ease. If that was possible under the circumstances.

Taking the seat next to her, Danthres folded her hands on the battered wooden table, which caused it to tilt slightly. Looking down, she saw that someone had removed the folded over parchment that had been placed under one of the legs to keep the table steady.

Ignoring the wobbly table, she said to Morenn, "First of all, let me apologize for Fanthral."

"Is he really hunting down lords for the latest attempt at an elven government?"

Danthres nodded. "Believe me, I don't want him here, either, but our captain forced him on us. It's bizarre, actually—they fought against each other in the war, and now they act like old friends."

Morenn regarded her curiously. "I hadn't realized there were any women in the Castle Guard."

"And I hadn't realized there were any women mages. So I suppose we're even."

"Are you the only one?"

"No." Danthres shook her head. "I'm the only one who has rank, however. Most of the ones we do have are assigned to Unicorn Precinct. The crimes there tend to be of a much less violent nature."

"As if we can't handle ourselves." Morenn snorted. "Men may be larger, but women, in my experience, fight nastier."

Danthres chuckled. "If you don't mind my asking, how did you become a mage?"

Morenn rolled her eyes. "So many have asked me that. It's like asking you how you came to have blond hair. It wasn't as if I had a choice. My facility for magic was obvious early on." She leaned back in her chair. "I was an orphan in Velessa, raised by Temisan monks. They saw my potential, and trained me as best they could, but religious magic is minor at best, so they sent me to the local brotherhood representative."

Danthres held up a hand before Morenn could go on. "Let me guess—an old man with a superiority complex, a dismissive tone of voice, and who never even looked at you when he spoke to you?"

That got Morenn to laugh. It was quite musical and pleasant, very much a higher-pitched version of Torin's. "How *ever* did you know that?"

"Please. We're on our second brotherhood representative. On the face of it, Gunderson is nothing like Ythran, yet in all the ways that matter, they're exactly alike."

Morenn nodded. "In any case, this wizard—his name was Vastar—simply said, 'Women cannot wield magic,' and teleported me away. So I went to see him again, this time casting a spell right in front of him. He said that anyone can buy a spell and pretend to cast it. I tried four more times, but he refused to even acknowledge me." She sighed. "How did you manage it?"

"Well, there's no actual proviso *against* women in the Castle Guard. It wasn't easy, mind you, but the fact that I don't give a shit what anybody thinks of me helps immensely."

"I can imagine."

Danthres smiled. "And, to be fair, I had help. Captain Brisban was in charge when I signed on, and he was miserable, but after he died the death he so richly deserved, Osric took over, and he almost immediately promoted me. Ten years later, he considers my partner and I to be his top detectives, and the shitbrains I served with in Goblin back in the day are either still guards or retired or dead."

"Living well can be a good way to get back at those who wrong you," Morenn said while nodding sagely. "That's why I created Bliss."

Grateful that she had led the conversation there without Danthres having to push it, she asked, "I was going to ask about that. Why *did* you create Bliss?"

She leaned forward again, resting her elbows on the uneven table. "I wanted to prove that my magic could be good for something. It took me *years*—with some help from the Temisan monks, priestesses, and priests—to teach myself magic. One in particular was very helpful, a cleric named Genero."

Danthres rolled her eyes.

"You know Brother Genero?"

She nodded. "Torin and I handled the murders of Gan Bright-blade, Olthar lothSirhans, and—"

"That was *you*?" Morenn went wide-eyed.

"Yes, it was us," Danthres said pointedly. While she knew damn well how good she was, she also knew that she was better with Torin—and, conversely, that he was better with her. "Genero spent most of the time hindering our investigation."

Morenn grinned. "Let me guess—he thought he was doing it for your own good?" At Danthres's nod, Morenn said, "Of course. I'll always be grateful to Brother Genero for his aid, but he is a bit full of himself."

"A bit? He's so full of himself, there are practically two of him. He and what remained of that little band of heroes didn't even leave town until after midsummer, and before they did . . ." Danthres shuddered at the memory.

"In any case," Morenn said, "I simply wished to prove that

magic could be used to help people, and that I could make a contribution."

Danthres stared at her. "*That* was your goal?"

"Of course. I wanted to give people something that would make them happy."

"Yes, so happy that they continue to take the drug in higher and higher quantities until they can't handle it anymore." Danthres tried to keep the harshness out of her voice, but the thought of Hawk made that hard.

Wincing, Morenn at least had the good grace to sound abashed. "I know, I know. I'm *trying* to perfect it, and I'm getting close, but I need the right components. Once we get the money from Gavin—"

"Gavin?"

"It was a deal Kempog brokered with that sycophant of his, Urgoth." Morenn shuddered, not hiding the contempt she felt for her partner in drug distribution. "Gavin was going to take a massive shipment onto the sea. He's supposed to pay us today, actually."

Danthres stood up, not willing to let Morenn see her anger just yet. With that one name, the wizard managed to piss away a great deal of the good will Danthres had toward her.

Then she turned around, and Morenn recoiled from the fury in Danthres's expression as if the lieutenant had slapped her.

"Do you know how Gavin was raising that coin?"

"I don't—"

"He robbed the Cliff's End Bank. Three robberies, in fact, just to pay for that big package of your precious drug. His third robbery, though, was somewhat less successful, and it ended with both Gavin and one of my fellow lieutenants being killed."

"What?" The word came out of Morenn's mouth as a croak. "Gavin's dead?"

"As is a detective in the Guard—and my friend."

Morenn blinked several times. "Lieutenant, I'm sorry, truly—I had no idea that Gavin was stealing the money, and I certainly had no idea it would lead to two deaths."

"Oh, more than that. Fanthral out there has a burr in his armor because he's supposed to bring Elthor lothSerra back to elf country. But he can't, because lothSerra took a considerable amount of Bliss, and then died. That, by the way, is how you were found out. If the ODs had continued to be people nobody important cared about, our M.E. would never have even known that Bliss was created with magic. But an elf lord died, so now we're all hip-deep in shit."

For several seconds, there was silence, except for the now-heavy breathing of Morenn, who was visibly upset by what Danthres had told her.

"Lieutenant, again, I'm sorry. None of this was what I intended. I'll be happy to turn myself in, and be tried on whatever charges there might be as relates to your friend's death and the theft at the bank."

"Would that it were that simple." Danthres started to pace the interrogation room. "The problem, Morenn, is that the Brotherhood of Wizards wants two things. The first is for you to eliminate all traces of Bliss."

The wizard's mouth fell open. "That's not possible."

"Really? I was under the impression that all spells can be counteracted."

Morenn nodded. "All right, it's *possible*, but it's a spectacularly bad idea. If I do that, the city-state will be overrun with depressed people desperate for more Bliss, and getting incredibly sick from withdrawal."

"Wonderful." Danthres rolled her eyes. "Somehow, I doubt that the brotherhood knows about that—or cares."

"You and I both know they don't." Morenn sighed. "What's the second thing they want?"

Danthres pointed at Morenn. "You. Back in those restraints. Probably to 'deal with' you."

Another shudder. "I'd rather stay here and face your magistrate's justice. I'm willing to admit that I was culpable in what happened with Gavin, and I'll accept whatever punishment is deemed acceptable. Better that than face the brotherhood."

Now Danthres just stared incredulously. "Are you *that* naïve? Do you honestly think that you—or I—have a *choice* here?"

"There's always a choice, Lieutenant."

"Yes, and you made yours when you decided to train as a wizard. It's not like it's a secret that the *Brother*hood of Wizards doesn't allow women. And you also *chose* to market a drug that, by your own admission just a couple of minutes ago, you haven't perfected yet. I went to the body shop the other day, and it is piled high and deep with Bliss ODs."

Tightly, Morenn said, "I have already told you, Lieutenant, I will accept the consequences of that action."

"And what of the other actions? You were told that the brotherhood wouldn't allow you to practice magic. In fact, you were— again, by your own admission to me just a few minutes ago—told *several times*. Yet you went ahead anyhow."

"Because the exclusion of women from practicing magic is ridiculous!" Morenn punctuated her point by slamming her palm on the table.

"Yes, of *course*, it's ridiculous. The world is quite well filled with ridiculous rules and laws and traditions, and sometimes it's necessary to protest them and declare their ridiculousness for all to see." Danthres walked over to the table and put her hands on it, leaning in to stare closely at Morenn. "But you also have to accept that such actions may have very serious consequences."

They stared at each other for several seconds. Danthres saw fear building in Morenn's eyes. She had obviously known intellectually what she had done, but now she was *feeling* what she'd done, right down to her bones.

Finally, Morenn whispered, "You can't turn me over to the brotherhood."

"Really?" Danthres straightened and barked a bitter laugh. "I've tried defying the brotherhood in the past, and it's never ended well for me. I've also seen them get what they want more often than not."

Morenn sat up straight. "When have they not gotten what they wanted?"

Smirking, Danthres said, "Like any organization, they have their issues. But they're very powerful, and their reach is long." She sat down and put a gloved hand on Morenn's hands, currently resting on her lap. "Look, Morenn, I have no wish to turn you over to those sanctimonious shitbrains, but I don't see that I have any choice. Do you?"

Silence greeted Danthres's question.

EIGHTEEN

UNDER NORMAL CIRCUMSTANCES, LADY MEERKA WOULD HAVE avoided this meeting at all costs.

She absolutely detested dealing with the politics of running the city-state. It always involved personalities and politeness and knowing who to snub and who to be nice to and so much other nonsense that she just couldn't bear it. She was willing to put up with state dinners—though even then, she insisted on staying at the main table with her daughters, since she understood how to talk to *them*—but that was as far as it went. Albin was good with people, and he knew how to form a consensus and make friends and compromise and all that other idiocy she had no patience with.

Given a choice, she preferred numbers. They didn't lie, or tell you one thing and do something else, or act nice to you when they didn't like you. Numbers made sense. They brought order to the chaos of life.

That was why she stuck with handling the city-state's finances. It made sense to her, and as an added bonus, she was very good at it. She had discovered the irregularities in the Hazlars' accounting, and brought it to Albin's attention. He then took it upon himself to exile them from Cliff's End—though it was done in such a way that they could save face, an effort Meerka would not have bothered with.

Now the Cliff's End Bank was the only bank in the demesne, which had concerned Meerka, but nobody had stepped up to open a new one, and the Grovises at least didn't try to embezzle money from the citizenry.

The events of the past two days were of great concern to Meerka, and she should have been meeting with Harcort Grovis and his brother Fentin to discuss what to do about these three robberies. While on her way to *this* meeting, a pageboy had informed her that the Castle Guard had captured the malefactors, so at least the money was likely to be recovered. But she needed to speak with them about security. Until Sir Rommett had informed her that the bank had discontinued their security system with the Brotherhood of Wizards, Meerka had not known about it. She had studied the Castle Guard's reports about such things, and robberies of the type recently perpetrated had a tendency to be repeated, and that was simply unacceptable on any level.

Of course, Harcort and Fentin were likely to come back to her whining about the loss of the promised investments from the Cynnis family, but it never should have gotten to the point where the infusion of capital from the Cynnises was required. Proper money management would have made that an added benefit rather than a necessity.

In any case, that had to be put off because Albin had been called into a meeting.

Normally, that wouldn't be an issue, but Albin was very ill. This wasn't his usual late-summer sickness, either, as that was usually improved after a few days. No, he'd been growing steadily worse, and the healers had no idea what to make of it.

And were the meeting called by anyone else, Meerka's response would have been to tell them to go away because the lord of the demesne was too sick to talk to anyone. But the meeting was with Gunderson, the new local representative from the Brotherhood of Wizards. One did not refuse meetings with the brotherhood.

So Meerka accompanied Albin to the meeting to make sure he didn't overtax himself. It had gotten so bad that Meerka had sent for their son, Blayk, to return from Iaron, where he'd been living with his wife's family for the past five years.

Besides Albin, Meerka, and Gunderson, present in the sitting room—with the fire blazing in a desperate and failed attempt to keep Albin warm—were Captain Osric and that elf general whom

Marta and Marcus desperately wanted them to all be nice to for no good reason that Meerka could determine. Gunderson was seated on the sofa, with Albin on the chair nearest the fireplace, Meerka in the chair across from him. The elf and Osric both stood.

The meeting could finally start when Boneen arrived. "My apologies for being late." He moved to join Gunderson on the couch.

That elf—whose name Meerka did not consider it worth her time to remember—spoke first. "Morenn must return with me to elven lands to stand trial for her crimes against the elven nobility!"

Boneen stared incredulously at the elf. "And what crimes would those *be*, exactly?"

"She is responsible for the death of a person of interest in the war crimes trials that I—"

"As I already told you," Boneen said testily, "lothSerra caused his own death. *He* took the drug."

"That woman is still responsible!" The elf was striding toward the couch now.

Osric pushed himself off the wall he was leaning against and walked over to the drinks table. "Fanthral, stop being an ass."

The elf—Fanthral—whirled on Osric. "I beg your pardon?"

"Beg all you want, you won't get it." The captain poured himself an amber liquid. Meerka had no idea what it was, as she avoided alcohol. It made her lose focus.

"LothSerra killed himself. If he'd done it with a dagger, we wouldn't arrest the smith who forged it."

Turning away from Osric, Fanthral looked at Albin, who just seemed miserable. "I warn you, Lord Albin, I was promised full cooperation by your monarchs, and if I do not receive it, you risk war."

"Yes," Osric said with a snort, "we risk war with a government that may not survive the year. We are quite frightened, I assure you."

"Are you mocking me, Osric?"

"Very much so, yes." Osric walked over toward the elf, and Meerka was worried that they'd start a fistfight. "It doesn't matter what crimes you *think* she committed. We *know* she's an accessory to three bank robberies and the murder of one of my detectives. She needs to go before the magistrate, and—"

Gunderson finally spoke. "Unacceptable. She is in violation of our primary bylaw."

"Well, that's not right," Meerka said.

Albin stared at her with a look that Meerka recognized as the one he gave her when she said something inappropriate. But to her mind, what Gunderson said was more inappropriate.

"Excuse me?" Gunderson said archly.

"I've studied the bylaws of the Brotherhood of Wizards on several different occasions, and I distinctly recall that the first one is that 'A brotherhood scroll that has been be-spelled must then be sealed with the brotherhood seal.'"

"The point is—" Gunderson started.

But Meerka wasn't finished. "In fact, there's nothing in your bylaws that says anything about not allowing women to be a part of the brotherhood."

"It's inherent," Gunderson said in a rather tight voice. "Women cannot be—"

"Brothers?" Osric asked with a smirk.

Gunderson stared witheringly at the captain. "Wizards, obviously."

Boneen looked at Gunderson as if the other wizard had grown another head. "I'm fairly certain she's conclusively proven that to be false."

Waving his arm dismissively, Gunderson said, "She may have learned a few minor tricks, but—"

"She created a magickal drug that has hooked half of Cliff's End, *and* she performed a Teleport Spell on a dozen people, with only moments to prepare, to a location she'd never been to before. That's not a few minor tricks, Gunderson, that is a *wizard.*"

"It doesn't matter." Gunderson looked away from Boneen and right at Albin.

Albin looked helpless for a second, so Meerka spoke again. "It does matter, actually. If there is no bylaw that women can't be mages, than you have no grounds for your objection."

Gunderson was getting very obviously angry now, which confused Meerka, as she thought she was clarifying the situation with her explanations. After all, if Gunderson wasn't familiar with the brotherhood's bylaws, he should be grateful that she was there to remember them for him.

"It is irrelevant!" he screamed.

Albin said in a croaking voice, "Please, Gunderson, if you would be so kind as to not shout."

Inclining his head out of respect, Gunderson spoke more softly. "My apologies, Lord Albin. But as I was saying, it is irrelevant. Regardless of her sex, this woman—"

"Her name is Morenn," Boneen said.

Gunderson gave Boneen another withering look. "Regardless of her sex, this Morenn woman is practicing unlicensed magic, and dealing with her falls within the brotherhood's purview." Now he transferred his gaze to Meerka. "*That* is in both our bylaws *and* in the legal code of your demesne."

Meerka blinked. "Of course it is. I already knew that, I don't see why you're telling me."

"But that's not always so, is it?" Osric asked. "Earlier this year, we had a wizard murdered named Efrak. He wasn't a member of the brotherhood, so you all refused jurisdiction, allowing my detectives to handle the case."

Boneen said, "Efrak was a special case, Captain."

"So is this!" Osric then looked pained, and glanced over at Albin. "Apologies for shouting, my Lord."

Albin inclined his head.

"One of my detectives is *dead*, and Morenn is partly responsible. What's more, she *admits* responsibility, and is willing to abide by whatever decision the magistrate makes regarding her fate. After her case is heard, we'll be happy to turn her over, once she has served whatever sentence is given her."

Gunderson raised an eyebrow. "And if she's put to death?"

"It seems to me that would solve all your problems, wouldn't it?"

A knock came at the door. "Come in," Albin said, sounding relieved at the interruption. For her part, Meerka wasn't at all grateful, as this would make the meeting take even longer.

Nuge, one of the pageboys, entered. "Excuse me, my Lord, but Lieutenant Tresyllione is outside. She says she needs to speak to you urgently."

"I'm afraid she'll have to wait until we're finished with this meeting, Nuge. Tell her to wait, please." Then Albin started coughing.

Once the coughing fit was over, Nuge said, "Begging my Lord's pardon, but she said that you might say that, and she said that if you did say that, to tell you that what she has to tell you relates directly to what you all are talking about."

Osric said, "I can assure you, my Lord, that the lieutenant would not willingly set foot in this wing of the castle unless it was urgent."

Albin sighed. "Very well, Nuge, send her in."

A very unattractive woman in Guard armor and an earth-colored cloak entered the sitting room. Based on the odd combination of features, she had to be the half-elven lieutenant, which matched the name spoken by Nuge.

"I'm sorry for interrupting."

Meerka frowned in confusion. Usually when someone apologized in this room, they sounded like they meant it. Lieutenant Tresyllione, however, sounded incredibly insincere. Meerka was glad to see that someone else hadn't gotten the hang of that, either, and she made a mental note to get to know this woman better.

She went on: "But I'm afraid I have some news. Morenn has killed herself."

"Really?" Gunderson stood up. "Well, Captain, perhaps you were right. Come, Lieutenant, let us see the body." The wizard shook his head. "I'm not surprised—women don't have the fortitude to handle adversity in such a manner."

Meerka saw Lieutenant Tresyllione's fists clench. Yes, she definitely would have to get to know her better . . .

NINETEEN

TORIN STOOD WITH HIS FELLOW MEMBERS OF THE CASTLE GUARD ON an empty dock. The early-morning sun glinted off the Garamin Sea. Ships were tethered to the docks on either side, but were relatively quiet.

All the detectives were present, along with Osric, and guards from all five precincts. The wooden planks groaned from the weight of so many armored figures standing on it, but the docks were built to withstand the weight of several hundred fish every day, so they would likely hold.

The unusual lack of activity was no doubt out of a combination of respect and fear. Illegal activity was more or less the order of the day on the docks, and the guards of Mermaid Precinct generally restricted themselves to dealing with the most heinous of crimes, and otherwise mostly just participating in the graft. A recent attempt to clean up Mermaid had failed rather spectacularly—but even so, the dockrats knew that today was *not* the day to be pressing their luck.

Dru stepped forward, holding an urn filled with Hawk's ashes. He turned to face the dozens of guards present. Off to the side were five civilians. Torin only recognized two of them: Hawk's father, who looked remarkably robust for a man who was supposedly so infirm that Hawk had to take care of him during off-hours, and a woman whose husband had been murdered a year ago. Hawk and Dru had caught the murderer, and Hawk and the woman had seen each other many times after the case was done.

"Hawk loved the sea," Dru said suddenly without preamble. His voice echoed off the boats in the adjacent docks. "He was gonna buy a boat, actually. Had been savin' up for years. It was seaworthy and everything. Right, Horran?"

Torin looked over to see Horran, a guard assigned to Mermaid, say, "You bet, Lieutenant. My guy wouldn't lie about that."

"Yeah." Dru smiled for a moment, then grew solemn once again. "When he was a kid, he wanted to be a sailor. His grandfather'd take him out on his merchant vessel, and he'd go on about how he wanted to join his crew. But after his grandfather died, and Hawk grew up, he decided to become a guard."

Dru looked around. Tears were welling up in his eyes.

"The shipping business's loss was our gain. He served as a guard, then got promoted when he helped Lieutenant Linder solve a murder right here on the docks, 'cause he knew stuff about boats that Linder didn't. Cap'n Osric kept an eye on him, and promoted him, same day he promoted me."

Osric nodded along with Dru's story.

"He was a great partner. I'd forget stuff sometimes, but he'd always pick me up. And he'd forget stuff, and I'd pick him up. That's what partners *do*, y'know? I hate that he's gone, but—" He wiped a tear away with a gloved hand. "Well, if he *had* to go, this was how he shoulda done it. See, staking out those banks wearin' glamours was *his* idea. He wanted to stop the thieves, and he did. He did it without anybody 'cept himself gettin' hurt. And he took one of those shitbrains down with him."

He turned to face the sea and pulled the lid off the urn. "Hawk wanted his ashes spread over the Garamin. So that's what I'm gonna do."

Tilting the urn, he shook it so that the ashes—which Torin assumed were created by the furnaces at the body shop—flew out onto the sea. The wind picked up, blowing the ashes all around, some of them even toward one of the other boats.

Osric walked up to Dru and put a hand on his shoulder. Dru turned to look at him, and they nodded to each other.

After that, the gathering started to break up. Torin looked

around for Danthres, and found her talking to one of the civilian women that Torin hadn't recognized.

As he walked toward her, Hawk's father grabbed his arm with a tight grip. "'Scuse me, but—you got yourself a brown cloak, so I'm guessin' you worked with my son?"

"Yes."

"Then can you be tellin' me—was Dru tellin' himself the truth? 'Bout my son?"

"Every word of what Dru said about Hawk was the truth, sir," Torin said solemnly.

Hawk's father let go of Torin's arm, for which the latter was extremely grateful. "So you mean to be tellin' me that that little ingrate was gonna be buyin' a damn *boat*? What was I supposed to be doin' while he was off gallivanting on some damn *boat*? Damn fool, he was. If his soul wasn't with Wiate right now, I'd be puttin' his ass over my damn knee."

He turned to wander off, still muttering expletives regarding his dead son.

Horran was standing near Torin, and he regarded the lieutenant with confusion. "Was that Hawk's old man?"

Torin nodded.

"Damn." Horran shook his head in disgust. "Some father, huh?"

"Oh, it could be worse," Torin said knowingly.

"Really?"

"Trust me," Torin said emphatically, then continued walking toward Danthres.

Just as Torin approached, the woman she was talking to was heading toward a boat. It looked to Torin like the *Breeze*. "Who was that?" he asked Danthres.

"A friend." Danthres shrugged. "Come on, let's head back. We've got paperwork to do."

Torin frowned. "You *hate* paperwork. Why are you suddenly so eager to do it now?"

"I just want to put this mess behind me so we can move on to the next case."

Everything Danthres said was reasonable, but something was

wrong with her tone. It wasn't anything major, just a slight lilt. Torin doubted that anyone else would have noticed it, but to Torin, it was a warning sign.

"Who was that woman?"

"Just—"

"The truth, please, Danthres. You're using the same tone you used three years ago when you got kicked out of your flat and wouldn't tell anyone."

Danthres let out a long sigh. "You know me too damn well." She looked around furtively. Of course, they were surrounded by their fellows, as well as the few sailors that were willing to brave the docks anywhere near this large a collection of guards.

"C'mon, walk with me." She started striding back toward the mainland.

It wasn't until they were walking down Meerka Way just past Jorbin's that Danthres finally spoke. "That was Morenn."

Torin stopped walking. "What?" he bellowed.

"She's getting on the *Breeze* and going somewhere far away."

"Danthres, I saw her corpse, however briefly. We *all* did. How did—?"

She held up a hand. "I'll explain. But can we keep walking? We're drawing attention."

Looking around, Torin saw that the people of Goblin, who generally minded their business, were staring a bit after Torin shouted.

"Very well." He started walking, Danthres moving alongside him. "How did she survive being a corpse in the interrogation room?"

"She never was one." Danthres smiled.

"Look, Morenn," Danthres had said in the interrogation room to the wizard, "I have no wish to turn you over to those sanctimonious shitbrains, but I don't see that I have any choice. Do you?"

Silence greeted Danthres's question for several seconds, before Morenn finally asked one of her own: "What if you give them what they want?"

"What do you mean?" Danthres asked, confused.

She held her hands out, palms-up. "Let's be honest, Lieutenant. They want me dead. They'll try to rip whatever they can out of me to find out how I managed to learn magic without their *precious* instruction, and then they'll kill me. We both know that."

Danthres nodded. She'd been avoiding stating it outright, partly because she wasn't completely sure it was the case, but it seemed pretty damned likely.

"So let's give them my corpse." Morenn was smiling, which concerned Danthres. "I can cast a spell on a body to make it appear to be me in every way, and cast a similar one on myself to change my appearance. They'll think I'm dead, I can go somewhere far away, and everything will be fine." She snapped her fingers. "Oh, and there are scrolls I've hidden in the house that have spells that will wean people off Bliss. I'll tell you how to find them in exchange for letting me do this."

While Danthres had to admit to liking the plan, it had one major flaw. "It can't be done. Remember what happened the last time you tried to cast a spell within these walls?"

"Shit." Morenn sighed. "I forgot about that."

"Boneen's warded this place tight." Even as she spoke, though, Danthres realized that there were other options, especially given the tenor of her conversation with Boneen before coming in. "But there might be an alternative. I'll be right back."

She left the interrogation room to find Boneen right where she left him. Fanthral was nowhere to be found, which suited her fine. "Boneen, how would you like to stick it to the shitbrains who dumped you here and refuse to listen to your wise counsel about how to deal with female mages?"

Boneen frowned. "You are aware, Tresyllione, that I was joking about turning a female mage male, yes?"

In fact, Danthres had assumed him to be utterly serious. "Answer the question."

"It depends on what you have in mind."

Danthres smiled. "Just casting two Alter Appearance Spells."

Torin shook his head. "So you took one of Boneen's corpses—"

"Not one of his," Danthres said emphatically. "Those all are part of ongoing cases. No, he went to the body shop to get one that was up for the firepit. Boneen cast both spells, and then he went to a meeting with the Lord and Lady. I followed a few minutes later with the news that Morenn had killed herself."

"And they believed it?"

Danthres snorted. "Gunderson was relieved. Osric was pissed, but then a couple of guards from Goblin showed up with Morenn's scrolls."

"That part I knew about. Sergeant Markon is coordinating with a bunch of local healers to get those spells to the Bliss addicts. It'll take a while for people to recover." Torin stared at Danthres intently. "That's something Morenn should be supervising."

"She couldn't stay here, Torin. The spell would fool Gunderson for a bit, especially since it all but gave him what he wanted, but if she stayed in Cliff's End, she'd run the risk of being discovered."

"So she gets away with murder?"

"Oh, stop it." Danthres sounded aggravated now. "She didn't kill Hawk, Gavin's buddies did, and they're going before the magistrate tomorrow. Kempog was the one who made the deal with Gavin, and he's already confessed to it now that he's lost his pet wizard. The accessory charge was just a way to try to keep her here that failed."

"So you found another one?"

"Yes! What, exactly, did I do wrong, Torin?"

Torin sighed. "Oh, any number of things." Before Danthres could harangue him further, he added, "But what would have happened had you not acted would have been far worse. Honestly, Danthres, I'm far more displeased that you neglected to inform me of any of this. Or that you weren't going to tell me until I caught you out."

"I *was* going to tell you."

At that, Torin glanced at her sidelong.

"I *was*!" Danthres clicked her tongue. "But I wasn't about to do it in front of everyone. When we had a moment alone together, I would've shared the story. Besides, you weren't there—you were helping catch Hawk's killer, which believe you me, was a nobler task than anything I was dealing with back at the castle. Why Osric stuck me with that—"

"Because Osric is one of the cleverest people I know," Torin said. "Who else would he put in charge of dealing with the only woman in a male-dominated job?"

Danthres blinked. "I must admit—I hadn't thought of that."

"Yes, well, that's why he's the captain."

"Indeed." She shook her head. "Y'know, I was in that meeting for only a minute, but—well, Lord Albin looked *awful*. He should've been in bed. And Lady Meerka was with him."

That surprised Torin. The lady of the demesne generally stuck to finances and avoided politics. "She must be worried about him."

They arrived back at the castle in due course. Torin noticed that the quiet he'd observed on the docks was present throughout the city-state. Nobody wanted to mess with the Castle Guard today, it seemed, which suited Torin fine. After everything that happened, they all could use a few calm days.

As they approached the castle, they saw Fanthral exiting it.

"On your way are you, General?"

Fanthral nodded. "My business here is done. The man I came here for is dead, and the woman responsible is also dead. I had hoped to bring her back, at least, so I would return with *something*. Instead, I return to the Consortium empty handed."

Danthres grinned. "Maybe you'll be lucky, and the Consortium will have fallen apart by the time you make it back west."

That earned her one final glower from the elf—but it only lasted a moment. "Lieutenant—I do recall one thing from my sojourn to Sorlin that might be of use to you. A member of the council, a half-breed like yourself, named Javian told me that he was also coming to Cliff's End, once his business in the south was concluded. He said that he was only three weeks behind me, which means he should be here some time in the next two weeks. Perhaps he will be able to provide you with the answers to your questions."

Danthres said nothing, but her mouth appeared to get smaller. Torin hadn't seen *that* look on her face in years, either.

"Farewell, Lieutenant ban Wyvald. It was a pleasure to be on the same side as you for a change."

Torin simply inclined his head, since the alternative was to give a reply, which would almost have to have been, "The pleasure was all yours" or something similarly snide. Again he found himself reminded of how bad an influence Danthres was on him.

They continued into the castle. "Who is this Javian?"

"Among other things," Danthres said in a low voice, "he's the person responsible for my exile from Sorlin."

Before Torin could query her further on that, Sir Rommett, the demesne's chamberlain, entered the castle's grand entrance from the western side. He looked almost physically ill.

He looked so bad that even Danthres looked concerned, and Danthres hated Sir Rommett with a deep, abiding passion.

"Sir Rommett," Torin asked, "are you all right?"

The chamberlain shook his head. "No. None of may ever be all right again."

"What's wrong?"

"Lord Albin is dead."

TO BE CONTINUED IN *GRYPHON PRECINCT*

ABOUT THE AUTHOR

Keith R.A. DeCandido introduced Lieutenants Torin ban Wyvald and Danthres Tresyllione of the Cliff's End Castle Guard in *Dragon Precinct* in 2004 (reissued in 2011). They returned in *Unicorn Precinct* as well as short stories in *Murder by Magic, Hear them Roar, Bad-Ass Faeries, Pandora's Closet*, and *Dragon's Lure*. Those stories will be collected along with five new tales of Cliff's End in the upcoming collection *Tales from Dragon Precinct*. Rest assured, he's going to be diving into *Gryphon Precinct* soon enough. His recent and forthcoming work includes the *SCPD* novels *The Case of the Claw* and *Avenging Amethyst* (also fantastical police procedurals, but these taking place in a city filled with superheroes), the *Leverage* novel *The Zoo Job*, the *Scattered Earth* novels *Guilt in Innocence* and *Innocence in Guilt* as well as several pieces of short fiction in that universe, the opening novella in the thriller series *Viral* in collaboration with Steven Savile, writing the monthly *Farscape* comic book in collaboration with series creator Rockne S. O'Bannon, and short stories in *More Tales of Zorro, Liar Liar, Tales from the House Band, Bad-Ass Faeries 4: It's Elemental,* and *V-Wars*. All told, Keith has written more than 40 novels, dozens of short stories, and many comic books, with plenty more to come. Find out less at Keith's web site at DeCandido.net, which serves as a portal to his blog (kradical.livejournal.com), Facebook (facebook.com/kradec), Twitter (@KRADeC), his podcasts (*The Chronic Rift, Dead Kitchen Radio: The Keith R.A. DeCandido Podcast, Gypsy Cove*, and the Parsec Award-winning *HG World*), and his band the Boogie Knights.

The books that put the Dark...

MYSTIC INVESTIGATORS:
9780979690143
BULLETS AND BRIMSTONE
9780982619735
and
FROM THE SHADOWS
Patrick Thomas
9781937051228

SOUL BORN
9780983099321
BLOOD DIVIDED
9781937051242
Kevin James Breaux

HERE THERE BE MONSTERS
John L. French
9780982619773

WHERE ANGELS FEAR
CJ Henderson
and
Bruce Gewheiler
9780982619711

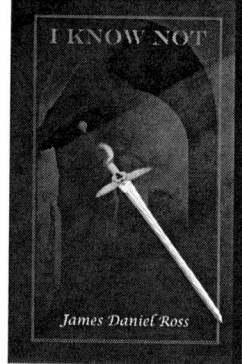

DRAGON'S LURE
Danielle Ackley-McPhail
9780982619797

I KNOW NOT
James Daniel Ross
9781937051105

FELL BEASTS
Ty Schwamberger
9780983099376

GET HER BACK!
David Sherman
9780983099345

VAMPIRE CAREER
Phoebe Matthews
9780983099369

STO'S HOUSE PRESENTS...
BEER WITH A MUTANT CHASER
KT Pinto
9781937051297

Please see our website for further details www.darkquestbooks.com

New Releases...

DRAGON PRECINCT
9781937051280
UNICORN PRECINCT
9781937051150
Keith R.A. DeCandido

THE HALFLING'S COURT
Danielle Ackley-McPhail
9780979690167

LEGENDS OF LONE WOLF
Joe Dever and John Grant
9780982619704

DEATH, BE NOT PROUD
edited by Thomas A. Erb
9781937051143

IN AN IRON CAGE
Danielle Ackley-McPhail
Elektra Hammond
and Neal Levin
9780982619742

RIVER
edited by Alma Alexander
9781937051235

The Eternal Cycle Series
YESTERDAY'S DREAMS
9781937051075
TOMORROW'S MEMORIES
9781937051082
TODAY'S PROMISE
9780983099345
Danielle Ackley-McPhail

LADY OF SEEKING
IN THE CITY OF WAITING
Jennifer Brozek
9780982619766

VAMPIRE DISASTER
Phoebe Matthews
9781937051259

CORPSE FAUNA:
THE DEAD BEAR WITNESS
James Chambers
9781937051259

AWFULLY FAMILIAR
Michael J. Tresca
9781937051532

CPSIA information can be obtained at www.ICGtesting.com
Printed in the USA
BVOW07s0154050914

365458BV00023B/143/P